Honor Thy BOSS

Love Ain't Easy

A NOVEL BY

CHARMANIE SAQUEA

ACKNOWLEDGEMENTS

First, I would like to thank God for blessing me with the talent of being an author. Here I am, on book number thirty-four; none of this would have been possible without him.

To my mommy, Sheree, who has been by my side since day one: you told me I could be anything I wanted to be if I put my mind to it. You have always been my backbone, and I would not have made it this far without you. Also, my Grammy, you've been there every step of the way, and I can't thank you two enough.

A HUGEEE thank you and shout out to Porscha and everyone at Royalty—you all are awesome! The love and support are miraculous.

I definitely can't forget to thank all the loyal readers who have been riding with me since Official Girl. You guys have been my motivation to keep going and busting my pen. All the inboxes, comments, and wall posts have never gone unnoticed, and I appreciate them and you more than you will ever know.

Last but never least, my Angels in heaven—Cora (Mom), Romney (Riggz) and Marisa, Uncle Tyrone (Big Shep), and Dad. I pray that you continue to watch over me. I can't forget my cousin Tyrein. Keep your head up baby; 2034 will be here before you know it.

Boy Meets Girl...

Boss

"I'm on my way," I spat into the phone.

With the speed of a man on a mission, I made my way to my car while simultaneously loosening my tie. Hitting the locks on the new Audi I had purchased, I snatched the damn tie off, throwing it in the passenger's side as I jumped in my vehicle. Not even giving a fuck that I was burning rubber, I sped out of the car's previous parking space.

With the precision of a NASCAR driver, I eased my way in and out of traffic as if there were no traffic guidelines or laws in place. My knuckles were damn near protruding out of my skin as I gripped the steering wheel while trying to remain calm.

Beeeep!

Obviously, somebody wasn't a fan of my driving and had no problems with letting me know as they proceeded to lay on their horn. I didn't even bother to give a fuck because I had much better things to worry 'bout. Not even fifteen minutes later, I was pulling up to my mama's like a lion on the prowl.

"She's gone, Boss," I heard her sweet voice say from the window she loved sitting in.

With a forced smile on my face, I walked into the house to find my nemesis and pain in the ass of a brother playing with my daughter while my mama sat in her favorite chair by the window.

"Daddy, you're early!" my five-year-old daughter, Giselle, exclaimed as she ran into my arms. "It's not even dark out, and you're here." She smiled brightly before blessing me with her kisses.

Hearing my baby girl say that caused my stomach to drop a little. It was true that in my line of business, I worked early mornings and late nights, but I never wanted Giselle to ever feel like I was neglecting her. From the moment that I found out I was going to be a father, nothing that I did was solely about me anymore. Every decision or move I made—I did it with my daughter in mind.

"You know Daddy can't stay away from his princess for too long. I had to come make sure you weren't driving your granny crazy," I told her before I started tickling her.

"Daddy, nooooo!" Giselle yelled through her laughter.

Our little moment was ruined by the sound of someone clearing their throat in a very aggressive manner. Sucking my teeth, I stopped my tickle attack on Giselle before placing a kiss on her cheek.

"Giselle, why don't you go finish picking up your toys in the playroom?"

"But I—"

"Hey, what do you do when an adult asks you to do something?"

2

I cut her off.

"I do it," she said through a pout.

"Get to it then."

Even though I deeply couldn't stand my brother, I was teaching my daughter to have manners and respect adults. At the same time, Giselle knew that if somebody grown told her to do something, and it didn't sound right—for instance, the whole good touch, bad touch scenario—she knew not to do it and come get me. I'd have no qualms about killing a muthafucka when it came to my daughter, no matter who it was.

"Well, at least you're teaching her something," my brother said smartly, and I just ignored his ass to keep from going in his jaw.

"Ma, you good?" I asked, directing my attention to my mama as she flipped through the channels on the new fifty-inch I had just bought her. "You need anything?"

"Boy, I don't know why you got me this big ol' thing, knowing I don't know how to work it," she fussed, ignoring my question.

"Because I was tired of seeing that box TV that you done had since you were a little girl," I joked as I pulled some money from my pocket and slid it into her hand, and she tried to quickly close mine to prevent herself from taking the money.

"Boss, I told. … Be careful, okay?"

My mama knew there was no point in trying to fuss at me about giving her money. Every day, I was sliding her some money or 'accidentally' leaving it somewhere in her house when she refused to take it. My mama was the type who didn't like people doing things for her if she felt she didn't do anything to deserve it. I always found myself explaining to her that I do what I do because she *did* what she did for me growing up.

No, all the money in the world couldn't amount to what she did for me, but she spent years of her life taking care of me. Now, it was time that I reversed the roles and took care of her.

"Always, I'll be back to get Princess later," I let her know before heading towards the door.

"We need to talk," my brother called after me.

"We don't have shit to talk about, Hendrix," I said dryly.

"I think we do, *Boston*! That's her mother; you can't keep Giselle from her."

I just shook my head and sighed because that was just like Hendrix—always sticking his fucking nose where it didn't belong and always worried about the wrong shit. The things that his punk ass should've been worried about, he liked to turn a damn blind eye to.

"Mind yo' damn business. That's not for you to worry about," I spat.

"It is when you got this shit popping up at my mama's house! You supposed to be the man in the streets, but you don't even have shit in order on the home front," Hendrix yelled.

"Hendrix, you—"

"It's cool, Ma. Let him say what he got to say," I cut her off as I stood there coolly.

I had never been the type to get out of my character unless it was required. I was always known for being cool, calm, and collected in any situation. Losing my temper was a rarity, and the shit Hendrix was spitting didn't call for the occasion.

Hendrix and I were complete opposites for us to have grown up in the same household and share the same parents. Hendrix was always a scholar of the sorts—never missed a day of school, never got anything lower than a B, and always had his head in a book. Hendrix had a lot of qualities, but being cut out for the streets was not one of them. I knew it, he knew it, and even our pops knew it when we were growing up; that was why he started preparing me when I was young.

He said he saw something in me that he didn't see in his oldest son. That didn't mean he loved him any less; it just meant Hendrix didn't have that it factor, and he hated it. Hendrix and I weren't always at each other's throats. We actually used to be close, but the moment Pops started schooling me about the streets, I started noticing some animosity coming from my big brother. Hendrix tried so hard to prove that he could be street that it was pathetic. One day, he finally realized he couldn't join me at this street shit, so he'd rather beat me at it and become one of the boys in blue. Who would've ever thought his sorry wannabe-hood ass would become a cop?

"Gianna needs help, Boss. You can't just toss her off to the side like that. Think about how Giselle would feel once she realizes that her daddy sells the very thing that her mommy is addicted to."

"Hendrix, don't do that," my mama warned him.

"And exactly how are you going to help her, Hendrix? By sticking your dick in her, right? Because that seems to be the way you always helped her when I wasn't around," I said, still remaining calm.

I could tell by the tightening of his jaw that Hendrix wasn't feeling me right now, but I didn't give a fuck. He wasn't as smart as he thought he was if he was walking around, thinking that I didn't know he was fucking my baby mama when we were together. I easily could've put a bullet in his head as well as hers, but what the fuck for?

Both of those dumb bitches were going to get theirs, and I wanted them to suffer in the worst way possible. Karma was already fucking Gianna; that bitch had a monkey on her back that she couldn't shake off, and until she did, she was not allowed anywhere near my daughter. I knew that karma had something very special in store for Hendrix's bitch ass, and I sure as hell couldn't wait.

"Exactly what I thought," I said once I didn't receive a response from Hendrix. "Since you're so concerned with the bitch, get her ass off the streets and clean her up because I don't have shit for her. And another thing, let this be the last time you worry about what the fuck I got going with my home front or any other front for that matter. What I do don't concern you, nigga," I let him know before finally making my exit.

I was tired of Hendrix trying to stick his nose where it didn't belong. What the fuck went on between the mother of my daughter and I should've been the least of his worries.

§

Checking my surroundings, I hit the lock on my car before walking up to the rundown house that looked as if it should've been condemned. I shook my head at the shit I was doing. Never would I have thought that shit would've come to this.

Lifting my hand, I knocked on the door before stuffing both of my hands deep in my pockets. I slightly turned my head and let my eyes roam over the street once more as I waited for someone to answer the door. Even though I was confident that no one was crazy enough to try me, I never was the one to be *too* cocky in any situation.

Moments later, the door cracked open, and a head poked out before it was fully opened.

"H-hey, Boss," Gianna said softly while rubbing her right hand up and down her left arm as if there had been a chill in the air.

Even after being strung out on drugs for the past three years, it was hard to deny Gianna's beauty. She had her hair pulled back in a tight bun on the top of her head, her skin was clear, and she had gained some weight since the last time I'd seen her.

"You clean?" I questioned dryly.

No matter how beautiful Gianna was, the love I once shared for her was gone. Finito. Never coming back. She had done one of the worst things you could do to a nigga like me, and that was cross me and make me lose my trust and respect for her. Most people would say that I was a hypocrite for getting mad at her for getting hooked on drugs when I flooded the streets with them, but that shit was different.

Gianna chose to start doing drugs because she couldn't live with the guilt of the dirt she had done. The day I busted her ass out for fucking my brother behind my back was the day that her life started going downhill. Had it been any other nigga, I would've just charged that shit to the game, not even tripping that hard over it. Before Gianna came into my life, I had a reputation for running through bitches. I was the type of nigga that could fuck six different bitches a day, seven days out of the week, just for the simple fact that I could.

If a bitch was throwing the pussy at me, why not catch it?

But when Gianna came into my life, a nigga was hit with the karma I should've known was coming. I fell hard for her ass with no safety net, and she stomped all over a nigga's heart like it wasn't shit. If nothing else good came out of our six-year relationship, Giselle did. If it weren't for my Princess, a nigga would've probably been doing life behind bars right now.

"Yeah, I been clean for almost four months now," she said with a small smile on her face.

Still unmoved by her revelation, I kept my firm stance while still glaring at her.

"How long is it going to last this time?" I spluttered.

See, this wasn't Gianna's first time getting clean. When I first found out that she was on drugs, I tried getting her some help and sending her to rehab off the strength of my daughter. It was a waste of time and money because her dumb ass didn't even stay there a full forty-eight hours before she ran off. That was just the first time; she had relapsed a total of three times already, so I wasn't necessarily being an asshole about the fact that she was claiming to be clean, especially when we had been through this rodeo too many times before.

"For good this time, Boss. I'm trying; I really am," she said as if she really believed herself.

"So, you stopped by my mama's, huh?" I switched the gears on the conversation.

"I just wanted to see her. I haven't seen my baby in three years. I miss her. This time is going to be different, I promise," Gianna said as if she were pleading.

The first time Gianna relapsed, I told her she was forbidden from seeing Giselle since she thought that the drugs were more important than the very thing she brought into this world. I would go to the end of this earth to protect Giselle, and since Gianna didn't feel the same way, why would I allow her around my child just to hurt her and bring pain into her little, young life?

"The only reason I'm not going to put my foot up your ass is I can see that you're off the drugs for now and didn't show up looking like a fucking zombie. When I say don't fucking come around my daughter, I mean that shit. If you want to see Giselle, you know what to do and how to get into contact with me. Don't go disturbing my mama with that bullshit."

"I'm sorry," she solemnly said with her head down.

Knowing that I got my point across, I turned on my heels to make my exit. I had been here longer than I'd planned to. If Gianna could stay clean this time, I had no problems with her seeing Giselle. It was never my intentions to keep my daughter from her mother, but I refused to let Giselle see her mother like that. She was getting older now, so that meant she was getting curious and asking questions that I didn't want to have to answer.

"Hey, Boss," she called after me. I slowly turned around to see what she wanted. "You know he meant nothing to me, right? I-I was just being stupid. I love you; I always have," she said as she started rubbing her arm again.

I scoffed out a reply before getting back in my car. The fact that Gianna thought I gave a fuck about that bullshit was beyond me. The shit she pulled was in the past, and I was over it—had been over it, but it was always going to be fuck Gianna from here on out. None of that had changed.

Choyce

"*Ugh*, this nigga's supposed to be making all this money, but his trifling ass still living in the fucking hood," my best friend, Jamaica, said as she slowed her car to a halt.

I sighed in annoyance because this was the last place I wanted to be. Putting my pride to the side, I dragged myself from the car and walked up to the door with Jamaica right behind me. I knocked on the door as if I were the damn police before crossing my arms over my chest, bouncing my leg anxiously. After a few moments with no answer, I banged on the door again.

"Who the fuck—what is you doing here?" Turelle asked angrily with a deep scowl on his face as he scanned outside like he didn't want anyone to see him.

If there had been an award for the world's worst baby daddy, it would've been for this no-good ass nigga standing before me. Four years later, and I was still trying to figure out what in the hell possessed me to have a baby by this nigga, let alone pay him any attention.

I was young; yeah, that's what it was. I was just going to chalk it up to the fact that I was just a baby and didn't know any better.

"I need some money for your daughter," I said as if it pained me to say so.

Under normal circumstances, I wouldn't have been asking his trifling ass for shit, but I was tired of his ass acting as if my child didn't exist. He was supposed to be getting all this money—buying different cars, more watches and chains than he did drawers, tricking off with this one and that one—but Zamani hadn't seen a penny from him in her four years of being on this earth. Hell, she hadn't seen *him* for that matter.

"Bitch, I know good and damn well you ain't bring yo' stupid ass over here with this shit!"

"Bitch?" Jamaica and I harmonized.

Not only was Turelle a deadbeat, but he was disrespectful as fuck. He had no problems with talking to me any type of way whenever I was in his presence. I saw Turelle at least once a week on the weekends when he frequented the club I worked at. Nobody—and I do mean *nobody*—knew we shared a child together or even knew each other. If Turelle wasn't straight up ignoring me as if he didn't know me, he was letting something foul shit fly out of his mouth.

"Yo' ugly ass knows better than to come at me with this shit, Choyce. You were a fucking mistake that never should've happened, and so is that baby. Get the fuck on, man," Turelle said through his teeth.

"I was a mistake, but you refused to leave me the fuck alone and loved threatening me over other niggas." I rolled my eyes at his ignorance. "Whatever, Turelle, forget it." I waved him off to take my exit.

"Umm, I think the fuck not, Choyce! I done told you about letting this nigga get away with this shit. You're not Zamani's only parent, so you shouldn't be taking care of her on your own. Get on his ass!"

Jamaica growled, pissed off.

"Take yo' dumb ass on fo' I—"

"Before you what? You ain't gon' do shit because everybody knows you ain't shit but a bitch—always have been. The only reason you feeling yourself is because you kissing that nigga Boss's ass, and he got you working as one of his flunkies."

Before I even knew what happened, Turelle had reached back and punched Jamaica right in her face. My mouth instantly fell open in shock. It wasn't the fact that he hit her that had me perplexed; it was the fact that he did it out here for everyone in sight to see.

"Maica!" I screeched as I grabbed her just as Turelle slammed the door on us as if he didn't just hit a woman in broad daylight.

"Bitch, I'm going to have yo' bitch ass killed! You got the right fucking one! I swear, they gon' fuck you up!" Jamaica yelled at the top of her lungs as I dragged her back to the car.

Thankfully, Turelle didn't hit her hard enough to where anything was broken. I just shook my head at what the fuck had just taken place. I was so embarrassed. That was one of the main reasons I never told anyone who Zamani's father was or was so pressed for him to be in her life. I was ashamed of who I had laid down and went half on a baby with.

If I could go back and do things differently, I sure in the hell would. I never would've paid Turelle's ass any attention, and I damn sure wouldn't have let him take my virginity or impregnate me. By no means did I regret my daughter; I just regretted the circumstances in which she was made and who I'd had her by.

"Maica, I am sooo sorry. I don't know what the hell is wrong with him." I solemnly shook my head.

"Fuck him, Choyce. I'm happy my goddaughter doesn't know who his bitch ass is, so I won't feel bad about getting his bitch ass killed," Jamaica said with fury.

I just put my head in my hands before gently rubbing my temples and sighing deeply. Even though Jamaica was speaking from anger, I knew that she was serious as hell. Jamaica's older brother was caught up in some crazy ass shit and was quick to pull a trigger on anybody who disrespected him or his family. One time, Jamaica had gotten into a fight with this boy she was dating, and he gave her a black eye. Let's just say ol' boy disappeared without a trace and hasn't been seen since.

"I don't see why you keep letting that nigga disrespect you the way he does, Choyce," she continued her rant. "That nigga gets beside himself all the time, doesn't do shit for his daughter, and you just let the shit slide. It couldn't be me."

"And it's not you, Jamaica. What you want me to do? Curse him out every time we cross paths with each other? Put him on child support? Send somebody after him to take him out? What would be the point in doing any of that when it's not going to change shit? I can't force Turelle to do anything for Zamani, and that's been proven for the past four years. I've been taking care of my daughter on my own since I was sixteen years old, so why should I try to get him to do anything for her when he already made it clear that he doesn't want shit to do with her?" I spat, fed up with the whole thing.

"Whoa, all that attitude is not necessary. You're mad at the wrong person."

"I'm not mad at anyone—more like irritated that I even let you geek me up to come over here when we both knew how this shit was going to end. That was my bad, though. Next time, just let me worry about my own child," I let her know.

"Sure thing, captain," Jamaica said sarcastically before turning the music all the way up just to be petty.

I wasn't the least bit phased by her or her actions. Jamaica and I went through these motions at least three times a month. We would get mad at each other over nothing, but before the night was even over, we were acting as if nothing had transpired between us. That was just how our friendship was. There were no hard feelings on either end.

§

My eyes scanned the club as I noticed that the club was more packed than usual. I wasn't complaining, though, because that meant there was more money on the floor for me. Tossing back the last of my apple Cîroc, I slid the glass back to the bartender when I noticed there was a commotion coming from the other side of the room.

"What's going on over there?" I questioned as a squinted to see why every bitch in the club was gathered over in the VIP section.

"Girl, that fine ass nigga, Boss, and a couple of his boys are over there. You know every bitch in here trying to be the chosen one, especially if it means getting close to Boss's stuck-up, sexy ass," Buffy answered as she was fixing another drink.

"Not every bitch." I sucked my teeth even though I had never personally seen Boss, because that nigga was like a ghost or something.

You only saw him when he wanted you to see him, which wasn't that often. Him nor the company he kept were my type of crowd, so we were never in the same place at the same time. I had heard plenty stories about him, though, and he was surely the type of nigga you should stay away from.

"Girl, you don't even count. I knew something was wrong with you a long time ago," Buffy joked.

"Ain't nothing wrong with me, baby. I'm just not basic like the rest of these hoes," I said before removing myself from the stool.

Buffy just shook her head from side to side but didn't offer up a response. Since every broad in the club was trying to squeeze their way into the VIP area, I was going to make the money they were leaving on the floor. Twisting my mouth to the side, I took a quick glance around the club once more.

Years of working at the club gained me the knowledge most bitches didn't have. Just one look at a nigga, and I could tell if he was really getting money or not. Most of the niggas that frequented the club were not the ballers they portrayed themselves to be. Most of them were married, looking to trick off with a bitch for the night, or some lame ass nigga who couldn't get a regular bitch to look his way, so he came to the club to live out his fantasies.

Getting pregnant with Zamani at the age of fifteen and having her when I was sixteen caused me to hurry up and grow up. My mama wasn't shit and kicked me out of the house because she swore I wanted her perverted ass boyfriend, and that was how I even got caught up with Turelle's trifling ass. No matter how much that nigga tried to fake the funk, he worshiped the ground my little young ass walked on until I got pregnant with my daughter.

Thankfully, I had enough smarts to not spend up all the money he used to love throwing my way, so I had a little something saved, but that wasn't enough for me to survive off of, especially being pregnant. Jamaica's brother, who was like a brother to me, helped me by setting me up in my own apartment, and I never could've thanked him enough for that. Due to having my daughter so young, I was never able to graduate from high school, and the only option for me to make money to take care of Zamani was to start stripping.

Of course, I lied about my age at the time and said that I was eighteen even though I was sixteen. Nobody ever would've known unless I told it because my body had developed way before it was supposed to. Four years later, here I was, still at the club, shaking my ass just to put food in my daughter's mouth and clothes on her back because she had a trifling ass father that refused to do anything for her.

"Damn, bitch, fuck you standing there looking stupid for?" I heard, snapping me out of my thoughts.

Already knowing who the voice belonged to, I rolled my eyes in the back of my head and walked off, refusing to even acknowledge Turelle's stupid ass. For somebody who didn't want shit to do with me, he loved doing shit to get my attention.

Before I could even walk all the way off, I felt somebody grab my wrist. I quickly turned around with my face scrunched up ready to go off, thinking that Turelle was going to make me show my ass in this establishment tonight.

"Don't, …" my voice trailed off when I realized it wasn't my sorry ass baby daddy.

"My bad," this stranger said with his hands up in the air in mock surrender. "I just had to stop you because my homeboy wanted to apologize for coming out of his mouth and disrespecting you like that. Ain't that right?" he threw over his shoulder.

I was trying to focus on what he was saying, but the way he eyed me while licking his lips caught me off guard. Don't get me wrong, I was standing here with nothing but a thong on with my titties barely covered, so I was used to the lustful stares, but his was different. I couldn't quite put my finger on what it was, but it caused a light shiver.

Not to mention the fact that this nigga was fine as hell. I didn't usually go for the light skins, but little daddy was surely winning. His skin was glowing under the florescent lights in the club. I could tell he had some light-colored eyes, smooth, plump lips that looked as if they could eat you into oblivion, and a low haircut with waves on swim. And even though I wasn't that fascinated with tattoos, he made that shit look sexy. Especially the one next to his left eye.

Hearing a grumble from behind him, I slightly looked past him to where Turelle stood with his face all twisted.

"What, nigga?" the stranger asked as he turned around at the sound of Turelle grumbling.

"I'm sorry," Turelle huffed.

I had to stop myself from laughing at this pitiful ass sight before me. This couldn't have been the same nigga that had just punched my best friend in her face a few hours earlier. Fighting to keep a straight face, I shrugged the whole thing off.

"It's cool," I said before turning around to finish what I had been trying to do.

"Aye."

Slowly turning around, I lifted my perfectly arched right brow to see what Mr. Stranger could possibly want now.

"Where you going?" he asked.

"Uhh, to make some money," I said as if he should already know that.

"C'mon," he said with a slight head nod before walking off without making sure I was following him.

I jerked my head back a little as I tried to figure out who he was talking to. Running my eyes over him, I took note of the plain white polo shirt and dark jeans he wore. His outfit was simple, but he'd topped it off with some all-white Balenciagas and a small but slightly flashy gold chain.

Money.

My radar was going off, so like a lost puppy, I followed behind his ass. He led us over to the area all the rest of the birds were flocking at, grabbing my hand before escorting us into the VIP section. That garnered a lot of dirty looks from the rest of the strippers, but I didn't care. I was used to these bitches hating my guts.

It was a dark-skinned dude sitting on the couch, who had about six bitches flocking him with all types of bottles in front of him on the table. He looked at me like I was the last slice of cake as we walked past him. I was guessing he was the infamous Boss.

"Damn, B. Who that?" he asked.

"Mind yo' business, nigga," Mr. Stranger, who I now knew went by B, said as he kept it moving.

He led us over to a couch in the back of the section where it was one bottle of Rosé, two blunts, and about four stacks of bills all sitting on the table.

"You sure you don't wanna be up there?" I questioned.

"Nah, I let them niggas do them. I'm not with all that wilding out shit; I just came here to chill to shut them the fuck up," he said before picking up one of the blunts and lighting it. "What I need for you to do, though, is dance for a nigga. You can do that, can't you?" he inquired as he held up one of the stacks.

Just then, a throwback R. Kelly song came on as if the DJ could hear exactly what he was saying. I let the beat of the music take control of my body as he sat back, puffing on his blunt while the music crooned through the speakers. His ass was unquestionably in for a treat.

Temperature's rising, and your body's yearning for me

Girl, lay it on me. I place no one above thee

Oh, take me to your ecstasy

I turned around, bending over to grab my ankle while twerking my left ass cheek when I felt a firm slap before a bill was slid into the hem of my thong. Just as I was standing back up straight, my body was pulled down into his lap.

It seems like you're ready

Girl, are you ready to go all the way

I didn't know if this nigga was hiding a snake in his pants or what, but I let out a small gasp. Slowly winding my hips to the beat, I closed my eyes when I felt his breath on my neck before he tickled me with another bill from the front of my thong all the way up my body. Going back down with the same bill, he slid it in my thong, making sure he brushed against my southern pair of lips, causing me to shudder a little.

He grabbed a handful of my hair, pulling my hair back but not too forceful where he would hurt me as he slid another bill in my top, running it across my right nipple before exposing my entire breast.

"Damn," I heard him mumble as he twisted my nipple in between his pointer finger and his thumb.

I didn't know what the fuck was going on. It was as if another entity had taken over my body. I usually had a no-touch policy, but something about his aura had me doing shit I would normally have slapped a nigga for doing.

The moment was interrupted by the sound of gunshots.

Pow! Pow!

"The fuck!" his voice roared.

"B! B! We gotta go! This nigga Turk just got shot," the chocolate lil' daddy from earlier said as he rushed over to where we were. I looked over in his direction as I put my exposed breast back in my top, and I noticed a look of annoyance on his face before he licked those juicy lips and ran his hand down his face.

"This dumb ass nigga," he mumbled before getting up.

Noticing he left the rest of his money on the table, I stopped him.

"Hey, you left your money!" I called out to him.

He turned around with a sexy ass smirk on his face. "That's not mine; you earned it," he said before letting his eyes roam over me one last time before disappearing into the pandemonium of the club.

Looking back over at the money, I noted that they were marked in stacks of one thousand dollars each. That meant that I had made four stacks off one dance that I didn't even get to finish.

Who is that nigga?

Boss

I pinched the bridge of my nose to help keep my composure. It was a Saturday, which meant this day was strictly supposed to be dedicated to Giselle. Everyone knew all my phones were turned off, not to contact me, and no business was done on Saturdays, because this was the day I spent doing nothing but being a daddy and doing whatever the hell my princess wanted. Yet here I was in a meeting, trying to figure out who'd put two bullets in one of my dumb ass workers.

Turk was a stupid ass nigga that got on my nerves more than he should. He was loud as fuck and had a big ass mouth that he loved running, so that meant he made enemies easily. Finding whoever wanted this nigga dead wasn't going to be easy, but I had to get to the bottom of it because I couldn't have his stupid ass bringing any heat down on my operation or me.

"So you telling us that you don't know who would be wanting to come after you?" I questioned while still pinching the bridge of my nose.

He had been shot once in his side and once in his shoulder. I had one of my doctors stitch his ass up and let it be known that he was not to miss this impromptu meeting today. I didn't give a fuck if this nigga was uncontrollably shitting on himself. He better had strapped a fucking colostomy bag to his shitty ass and been in attendance since he was the reason we were all sitting here.

"The whole fucking Detroit. With his dumb ass," my right-hand man, Johann, grumbled.

It was no secret that Johann couldn't stand Turk. For the life of him, he couldn't understand why I kept Turk around and hadn't long ago gotten rid of him. The answer was simple. Turk brought in a lot of money; no matter how obnoxious, annoying, or a pain in the ass that nigga was, it couldn't be denied that he was one of my top money makers. That reason alone was what helped me look past all his bullshit up until now.

Sucking his teeth, Turk shifted in his seat before cutting his eyes at Johann.

"Not today, Han," I warned him not to start.

I was already pissed about my day with Giselle being fucked with; I didn't need these two going back and forth like some bitches to further piss me off.

"Nah," Turk answered.

"Nah, what? The fuck is a *nah*, nigga?" I raised my voice a little.

"I mean," Turk corrected himself. "No, I don't know who would be wanting to come after me," he said.

I was far from a dumb nigga. I could tell when somebody was lying to me from a mile away, and this nigga had just looked me dead in my eyes and told a lie. It was cool, though, because I had something for his ass.

"Cool, well, since you don't know, I'm going to put you on probation until you fucking figure it out. When you leave here, take yo' ass over there on 7 Mile. It's your first day back in the trap," I informed him.

"What?" he spat. "Come on, Boss! I make too much fucking money to be sitting in a fucking—"

"This meeting is adjourned," I cut him off. "Y'all, get the fuck up out my face." I waved them off.

There was no sense in Turk trying to plead his case. The shit was already said and done. Since his ass wanted to act like a little nigga, I was going to treat him as such and sit his ass in the trap with my little niggas.

"Aye, B. It looks like Turk here has a problem," Johann said at the fact that Turk was still sitting there with an ugly ass look on his face even though I had already dismissed his ass.

"Nah, that can't be the case, Han. He knows that he better take his dumb ass over there like I told him to because a problem with me ain't what he wants. Ain't that right, *Turelle*?" I asked.

"Yeah, … yeah. You right, Boss," he said as he got up and walked out.

"Pow," Johann said as he used his hand as a gun. "I'm just itching to put a bullet in his bitch ass. Everything about that nigga just rubs me the wrong way," he sneered.

I just groaned as a response because I knew if it weren't for me, Han would've been killed Turk's ass. To call Han trigger happy would've been putting it lightly. I swore that nigga dreamed about killing people.

I thought the fact that this nigga had enlisted in the army and had gone to combat would've tamed his crazy ass, but I think it fucked his head up even more.

"What's wrong with you, B? Too much tricking off in the club last night?" he asked with a knowing look on his face.

Thinking about last night's events caused a small smile to form on my face. I honestly wasn't the clubbing type and hated being in that type of environment. Especially with me being who I was, you never knew who was secretly plotting on you and just waiting to catch you slipping so they could take you out. I only went out last night because I was tired of hearing these niggas bitching about me stepping out with them.

It was safe to say that I was way out of my element last night, but I actually enjoyed it—up until Turk's bullshit caused my night to end early.

"Hey, they say it ain't tricking if you got it, and we both know I got it. Plenty of it," I shrugged.

"Oh, so that's why you left that thick ass chocolate fee four stacks. Because you just got it like that, huh?"

I couldn't help but lick my lips at the mention of the chocolate ass stripper that I chose to spend my time with and money on. I just so happened to walk up on Turk going in on her as I was making my way back from the bathroom, and that shit didn't sit right with me. I didn't give a fuck if her ass had been standing in the middle of the club butt ass naked, there was no reason for Turk to be coming at her the way he had. I don't know; I guess having my daughter changed my perspective on a lot of things.

"She was thick as fuck, wasn't she?" I smiled with flashbacks running through my mind.

"Nigga, I would've traded her ass for all six of them bitches I had on my dick, but you wanted to hold her ass like she had the fucking secret Krabby Patty formula," Johann cracked.

"Nigga, you stupid," I laughed.

"Real shit, I hope you at least got the broad's name," he stated.

I shook my head in the negative. Now that I thought about it, I hadn't got the name of the chick who got four bands out me just from one little ass lap dance. If she could do that just from a dance, I knew her ass would do some serious damage if she were to put that pussy on me.

Nigga, you tripping.

I had to shake that thought from my head because I knew that was never going to happen. The only way I was ever going to see her again was if I were to go back to the club, and that was dead. Besides, I wouldn't fuck her anyway. Not that I had anything against strippers—I respected any female that got hers—but that just wasn't my style.

"Nigga, you fucking up." Han shook his head. "Anyway, I'm out. I got some shit to check on unless you wanna roll."

Weighing my options, I said to hell with it. I already had a hell of a lot of making up to do to the lady of the house. I'd just stop and get her something special before I headed home today.

§

I followed behind Han as he led the way into one of our warehouses we had where we kept our product. We called this one Building M because this was where all the manufacturing or what I liked to call 'magic' took place. We had a team of women who we used specifically for cutting, cooking, and bagging our shit. We didn't do like most niggas where they did all that and sold the shit out the same house. Nah, we liked to operate a little differently.

"Hey, Boss," rang out throughout the warehouse.

"What's up, ladies?" I spoke, giving a flirtatious smile.

"Is this nigga the only one y'all see standing here? He ain't no fucking superstar. The fuck?"

"Nigga, we see you damn near every day. What we need to be excited about seeing you for?" one chick asked as she walked past us.

"Shut yo' ass up," Han said while slapping her on the ass.

I could tell by the school-girl giggle that she let out that they were fucking. Hell, Han had probably fucked three quarters of, if not all, the bitches in here. That was why his ass loved coming to check on them so much. It was an abundance of ass and titties everywhere.

Did I forget to mention that the only article of clothing all these ladies had on was a thong and a face mask? Yeah, it was just titties and ass flying all over the place. Of course, this was Han's idea, and even though it was a wild one, it had been working for us for years.

"Boss, can I talk to you really quick?" a mocha-complexion cutie asked me.

Looking at the perky set of titties she had on display, I slowly let my eyes travel up to her baby face. She looked as if she were fresh out of high school. That made me put a mental note in the back of my head to ask Han if he had been making sure everybody in this bitch was legal and of age.

"What's up?" I questioned.

"I know you have a strict no-days-off policy, but can I please have tomorrow off? My son has been sick, and I need to take him ..."

Her voice trailed off when I held my hand up for her to stop. I wasn't as cruel and heartless as people thought I was. Being a father myself, I knew kids got sick, and you couldn't control that shit. Being a parent should always come before anything.

Too bad some niggas and bitches didn't understand that concept.

"Take the day off, ma. Make sure little man is straight," I told her.

"Thank you so much." She sighed in relief before heading back to her task.

After making sure everything was running smoothly, Han and I headed back out to our cars.

"What you about to get into?" I asked him as I leaned against my Hummer that Giselle liked to call a monster truck.

"Some pussy," Han answered with a straight face.

Unlike myself, my nigga was still in his hoe phase, so all he thought about was pussy and money. Shaking my head at him, I reached for my door handle.

"Nigga, you need help," I told him.

"No, just pussy. All I need is some pussy," he shrugged. "What you about to get into?" Han asked.

"Shit, about to go spend a lot of money to make your goddaughter happy because I know she's going to have a funky ass attitude when I get home. That shit is terrible; if she ain't get shit else from Gianna, she damn sure got her attitude." I shook my head.

For years. I had been trying to figure out why God would be so cruel as to give me a damn daughter. Don't get me wrong, I loved my Princess more than anything, but a nigga like me would've preferred a son.

"Hell yeah, you better curve that shit now while you can. The last thing we need is another Gianna," Han spoke nothing but facts.

"I'm already knowing, nigga. Call me later, though," I told him before hopping in my truck.

Now that business for the day was taken care of, it was time to head home to the only lady besides my mama that could put a smile on my face. My princess: Giselle.

Choyce

I tapped my pen on the desk and bounced my leg up and down ferociously as I willed myself to stay awake. Now that Zamani was older, I'd decided to go back to school to get my GED. The fact that I not only had a child, but a daughter, who was looking up to me, made me want to do better for myself. Not just myself, but for Zamani as well. When she got older, I wanted my daughter to be proud of me.

The sound of my teacher's voice snapped me out of my thoughts.

"Don't forget, everyone, you have a test tomorrow, so make sure you study. Have a great rest of your day," she said, dismissing us.

Immediately jumping up, I gathered all my stuff, throwing it in my backpack while calling my best friend on FaceTime.

"Hey, girl, how was school?" she answered.

"It was, blah, and I can't wait until it's over," I told her honestly.

I had made a lot of mistakes in my twenty years of being on this earth, and if I could go back and do things differently, I would. Not dropping out of high school and graduating instead would've been one of the first things I would've done over. Another big thing would've been never letting a dirty dog like Turelle get into my head or my pants.

"I know, but just remember, this is for you and Mani," Jamaica told me, giving me some words of wisdom.

"You're right," I sighed. "Where's my little diva at?" I asked, referring to Zamani.

"Taking a nap. I took her to the park to wear her little ass out. Ain't no way a damn four-year-old should have that much energy."

"She ate already? My stomach is touching my back, so I'm about to stop and get me something to eat really quick and wanted to know if I should get her something," I said.

"Bye, bitch, because I feel like you trying me right now. You really think I would have my baby over here and not feed her?" Jamaica ranted.

I lightly laughed because if I knew one thing, I knew Jamaica didn't play when it came to her goddaughter. Since she didn't have any kids herself, she loved and treated Zamani as if she had birthed her herself. She had been by my side since before I even found out I was pregnant and was still by my side to this day. She was basically my baby daddy.

"I didn't mean—"

The beeping sound let me know that her crybaby ass wasn't trying to hear shit I said by hanging up on me. Shaking my head, I opened the door to my 2016 Dodge Charger before starting it up and pulling off. I vibed to the music of Detroit's very own Icewear Vezzo as I made my way to Coney Island.

Before I even knew it, I had reached my destination. Snatching my keys out of the ignition, I quickly got out of the car. Hitting my locks as I made my way into the building to grab myself something to eat. After placing my order, I moved to the other side of the room to check the abundance of texts I had missed while in school. Someone else walked in, but I paid them no mind as I texted back a stripper named Fantasy to decline her offer of doing a party with her.

I didn't play that doing private parties shit. Bitches getting beat and raped at those types of functions didn't just happen in books and movies; shit like that happened in real life.

"Damn, the conversation that good that you can't speak?" I heard from the side of me.

I looked up to find Mr. Stranger from the club standing there, eyeing me.

Lawd, have mercy.

That night in the club did his ass no justice. Being that it was daytime, and we were in the light, I could see him better. Saying that he was fine would've been an understatement. Just like that night, he was dressed simple in a black hoodie, dark jeans, and black red bottoms. I didn't know why, but for some reason, I was feeling really nervous standing next to him, especially with the way he was looking at me.

Even though he had the same look in his eyes that night, it was weird because I was fully clothed, yet he was looking at me as if I were a chocolate bar or something.

"Hey, how are you?" I spoke, not really knowing what to say.

"I—"

"Boss, you. … Oh, shit. Hey," his friend cut him off.

Boss? Oh, shit! Boss. … The infamous Boss?

"Hey," I spoke back.

"What you want, man?" Boss asked as if he were embarrassed or something.

"Not a damn thing. Do you, dawg." His friend smirked before walking back out the door.

Just then, my food came up, so I went to go get it. Just as he did that night in the club, he lightly grabbed my wrist to keep me in place. I turned around and gave him a questioning look. He ran his pink tongue over his lips, sending my mind into overdrive.

"Aye, hold up. Don't leave yet, aight? I wanna holla at you real quick," he said to me.

"Okay, I'll be out there in my car," I let him know before getting my food and walking out.

What were the odds that the nigga I was rubbing my bare ass on a few days prior to today would've turned out to be Boss? Detroit's most wanted, and I didn't mean by law enforcement. I didn't know what I had dreamed of, but he looked nothing like I thought he would.

Hopping in my car, I wasted no time going in on my food, scarfing it down. Just as I was taking the last bite of my hot dog, Boss walked out the door. He was looking around as if he were in search of something, so I stuck my hand out the window and waved him over. I couldn't help but lick my lips at the way he swaggered over to my car, commanding attention with every step he took.

"This bitch bad. This you?" he asked once he effortlessly slid in and closed the door.

"Yup, this all me," I beamed proudly.

"Yeah, this nice," he complimented once again as he looked

around. "This real. ... damn you greedy," he expressed once he noticed that my food was gone.

I let out a laugh because he just didn't know the half. I was greedy as hell and always eating something. I looked down at my empty food container and shrugged, feeling embarrassed now.

"Not greedy, just hungry," I corrected him.

"You mind?" he asked as he gestured to his food.

"Go ahead."

"Yo' nigga must take good care of you if you riding around like this," Boss stated.

I didn't know if I wanted to be offended or not. It felt as if he were trying to insinuate that I wasn't capable of taking care of myself, or I needed a nigga in order to have nice things.

"No, nigga. I do for and take care of myself. I don't need a man; I'm what a man needs," I let him know.

"So, you're single is what you're telling me?" he asked with a mouthful of food.

"Don't talk with food in your mouth; it's rude. But to answer your question, yes. I'm very single."

Listening to my advice, he took a second to make sure his food was completely chewed and swallowed before speaking this time.

"Damn, so you must be one of them crazy bitches," he said, causing me to look at him like he was crazy.

See, I knew, sooner or later. this nigga was going to do something to turn me off. I knew that anybody who found it in themselves to hang out with Turelle's trifling, no-good ass had to have the same mentality as him.

"Okay, so this is where I'm going to cut this shit short. Have a nice rest of your day," I told him as I hit the locks so he could let himself out of my car.

"The fuck I do?" he asked as if he really didn't know.

"Bye, Boss."

"C'mon, man. I know you not offended by what I just said? So, it's okay for y'all to call yourself bad bitches and all this extra shit, but the moment a nigga call you a bitch, you wanna act all high and mighty? Fuck outta here," he spat.

"Look, I gotta go get my daughter and you holding me up. Now, do us both a favor, and get out," I said with a full-fledged attitude.

"Fuck you then! I'm not about to sit here and fucking beg you. Fuck I look like? I guess the truth hurts, huh?" he ranted as he got out, making sure to slam my car door.

I skirted off, most likely leaving tire marks in the process. Everything I had been hearing about that rude bastard turned out to be true. Sure, he was sexy as hell, but he was cocky as fuck and thought he was God's gift to the world. He may have been used to bitches bowing down to him and kissing his ass, but I wasn't the one.

Turk

With a scowl on my face, I sat in annoyance as I watched these little niggas in the trap fuck off. It was week two of my demotion, and I was still pissed the fuck off about the situation. I was the one who had two bullets pumped into my body. Niggas came after *me*—not the other way around, yet Boss was acting as if I had done something wrong. Just thinking about that shit caused me to suck my teeth.

"Y'all shut that shit up!" I bellowed. "Y'all ain't nothing but a bunch of fucking kids in this bitch."

"And? Yo' mad ass in here with us, so that make you a fucking kid too," this little nigga named Zay said.

Ever since the day I walked in this bitch, his little young ass and I had been bumping heads. Not only was he that nigga Han's nephew, but he had a smart-ass mouth that I just couldn't deal with. He thought because his uncle was second in command, he could get away with murder if he wanted to.

Fuck yo' punk ass and yo' bitch ass uncle, too.

"I'm a grown ass fucking man, don't ever forget it," I said as I pointed a finger at him.

"You ain't shit. If that was the case, yo' overgrown ass would be out there putting in some grown man work and not in here with us kids, right? You know, since you a grown ass man and all that."

This nigga must've thought he was the comedian of the year or something with that line, as he gained laughter from the rest of these dumb ass niggas in the house. Usually, I would've brushed his little ass off, but he had been getting beside himself too much for me lately.

"Nigga, let me tell you something," I said as I grabbed him by his hoodie and hemmed his little ass up. "I been doing this shit since before yo' ugly ass daddy even shot you out his nut sack. I put in more work than anybody in this camp, including yo' punk ass uncle. I'm the one in these trenches every day—not Boss, and damn sure not Han. When you speak to me, you better put some muthafuckin' respect in yo' tone, or I'll—"

Pow!

My rant was cut short by the bullet that had whizzed past my head, barely missing my ear by millimeters. I dropped Zay and stepped back to see what the fuck had just happened when I noticed Han and Boss were standing behind me, and Han still had his gun pointed at my head.

"Or you'll what, pussy?" Han spat with fury in his ass.

During my little rant, I hadn't noticed that either of them had come in through the back. Once again, my dumb ass would've been caught slipping.

Letting out a little laugh, I stepped back from Zay. "We was just playing, Han. Fuck you doing all that shit for? Ain't that right, Zay?"

"Hell nah, we wasn't playing, bitch. You just came at me all types of crazy," his little rowdy, big-mouth ass said.

"Chill the fuck out, Zay," Han told him. "Fuck you doing with yo' hands around my nephew's neck like you don' lost yo' rabid ass mind fa?" Han spat towards me.

The whole time, he never lowered his gun, and I was starting to feel some type of way about it. Usually, Boss would step in and control his mans because he was a little off the rocker, but he just stood back, leaning against the wall, letting Han do his thing.

"Boss, get ya homie. He gotta know we can have a civilized conversation without the fucking artillery. I ain't got my shit pulled, so what he got his pulled fa?" I questioned.

Even though both niggas were crazy in their own way, I knew I had a better chance at talking some sense into Boss than Han.

Just shrugging his shoulders nonchalantly, Boss didn't bother to open his mouth with a response.

"Bitch, I'm right here. You speaking as if I'm not even in the room." Han cocked his gun.

"Get his ass, Unc," Zay instigated.

"Aye, y'all little niggas, raise the fuck up outta here real quick," Boss instructed, speaking for the first time. "Zay, that includes yo' bad ass."

I bit my lip to try to contain my anger. I was feeling like Han was tryna play me like I was some type of hoe or something. Since the first day I started working for Boss, he'd been doing and saying some slick shit, thinking somebody was supposed to be scared of him or something.

"Put the damn gun down, Han. I'm not about to let you shoot this nigga, and I just got this carpet shampooed," Boss said.

With a crazy ass smirk on his face, Han put the safety back on his gun before stuffing it back in his waistline.

"If you got a problem with that little nigga or anything he do, you take that shit up with me. I'm grown, and he's not—no matter how he acts. If I ever catch you coming at him crazy, I'ma turn yo' bitch ass into maggot food. I already been itching for a reason to take yo' ass out. Pow!" He sneered while using his hand as a gun before turning on his heels and walking out of the trap the same way he'd come in.

Nigga, yo' days are numbered, and you don't even know it.

Besides my stupid ass baby mama, I had never hated somebody as much as I hated Han's black ass. He walked around this bitch as if he couldn't be touched, but he had me fucked up. Unlike the rest of these niggas, I wasn't scared of him or Boss. Them niggas talked a good game, but when it really came down to it, they weren't 'bout shit. Just two corny ass niggas that hid behind an army full of niggas.

Boss

"*D*addy. ... Daddy. ... Daddy!"

"Hold on, Han. Yes, Princess?" I asked as I moved the phone away from my ear.

I tried not to laugh at the little ugly face Giselle had on her face. Even though I hated it, more and more each day, she was starting to remind me of her mother. The little attitude she had developed was out of this world, and Lord knew I wasn't ready.

"Can we go get some ice cream?" Giselle asked in that sweet little voice she used whenever she wanted something.

"I just bought you some superman ice cream two days ago because that's what you said you wanted. I'll fix you a bowl in a minute," I told her.

"But Daddy, I want a ice cream *cone* dipped in chocolate, and we don't have that. You always say if I want something, just ask, and Daddy will make it happen."

I sat there with a blank expression on my face because I just couldn't believe that I had a little con artist on my hands. I didn't know whether I should've laughed or not, because Giselle was surely a slick one. She may have had her mother's attitude, but that slick shit was all her daddy. Not boasting or anything, but I was slicker than a can of oil.

"Han, please tell me you hear this shi-stuff," I chuckled lightly.

"Oh, I hear it, B. It seems to me like yo' ass 'bout to be going on an ice cream run. Gi-Gi not playing with yo' ass," he laughed.

"Ha-ha, very funny. You not gon' be laughing when I pack a bag and send her ass to you for a few days."

"Oooh, yes, Daddy Han!" Giselle yelled with excitement with a big smile plastered over her face.

Ain't that some shit.

My mouth fell slightly ajar at the fact that my daughter was so eager to leave me. Don't get me wrong, Han was her godfather, and I knew for a fact that he loved Giselle just as much as I did. Just like me, there wasn't anything in this world that he wouldn't do for my daughter, and I couldn't have picked someone better to be her godfather. It was just the fact that Giselle was my world, and I had technically been her only parent since she'd been on this earth, so I was very protective over her and slightly jealous whenever she left me for somebody else.

"See that? My baby don't mind coming to kick it with Daddy Han. She knows we'll fuck shit up. That's my little ace, so go right ahead and pack that bag, nigga," Han told me.

"Nigga, I'm not about to let you corrupt my daughter. The last time she spent a few days with you, she came back, talking about Molly, Percocet. Chase a check; never chase a bitch."

Han burst into laughter as if that were the funniest shit ever. It never failed; every time Giselle spent time with her godfather, she came back saying some crazy shit she picked up at his house. See, I was trying to be cautious about the things I did, said, and listened to around Giselle because I understood that she picked up on things quickly. Of course, I slipped up every now and then, but I was trying. Han, on the other hand, just didn't give a fuck. He said whatever flew out of his mouth around Giselle. One thing I would give him was he would never light up a blunt around my daughter.

At least his ass can do one thing right.

"Corrupt? Nigga, it sounds like she came back saying some real shit."

"Bye, Johann. I'll call you later, nigga." I hung up before he could say anything else.

When I looked up, I noticed that Giselle was no longer playing with her barbies and shit, but she was now looking at me with a quizzical look. Right then, I knew her little curious ass was about to ask me some shit. She literally had a question for everything, and I, being myself, always had an answer.

"Daddy, I thought you said that black men are not niggas. They're black kings. So why you call Daddy Han a nigga, daddy? He not a king?" she asked as if she were really trying to figure out if he were a king or not.

My heart swelled up in my chest at her saying that. Being a single father of a daughter wasn't the easiest thing in the world, especially when you were in my profession, but I took pride in the way that I'd raised her. No, I wasn't perfect by a long shot, and I didn't pretend to be, but as long as I taught Giselle some good, and she learned something positive from me, I'd done my job.

"You're right, Princess, but sometimes, us black men can act like niggas, and you have to call them what they are. You're my princess, though, right?" I asked as I swooped her up in my arms before placing kisses all over her face.

"Yes, Daddy! Yes!" she yelled through her laughter.

"Okay, now go get your shoes on so we can get your ice cream," I instructed.

"And burger," she added.

"What? You didn't say—"

"You always say I have to eat before dessert, Daddy. That's what you say," Giselle quickly said before turning around and running up the stairs.

That damn girl is going to be the death of me.

§

After stopping by nasty ass McDonald's to get my princess a burger like she'd asked, we found ourselves chilling in the car outside of Dairy Queen with the chocolate dipped cone she'd wanted so damn bad.

"Don't get that chocolate on Daddy's seat," I told her as I sat some napkins in her lap.

"I know, I know."

"Your Nana is going to have to do something to this head of yours when you go see her tomorrow. I know you're tired of wearing this damn ponytail," I said as I rubbed her head.

Even though Giselle was five years old, I hadn't mastered the whole 'doing hair' thing. I didn't have the patience or the time for that shit with me constantly having to check on some grown ass men like they were fucking toddlers. I had just learned how to do a ponytail a few months ago, and that was all Giselle let me do since she claimed I hurt her head. When it came to my mama, though, she sat there so quiet and peaceful like it was nothing with her little bratty, spoiled ass.

"I like when Nana does my hair; she makes it feel good."

"You're a hater," I laughed.

"Daddy?"

"Yes, Princess?" I asked.

"What's a crackhead?" she asked while licking away at her ice cream as if what she'd asked was no big deal.

I had to adjust myself in my seat and look at her for a few to make sure I had heard her right.

"Where you hear that word from?" I asked calmly.

"Uncle Hendrix and Nana were fighting, and he said it's your fault that my mama a crackhead. Half the city, too. Uncle Hendrix said he hopes Nana is ready to take me when you go away because it's going to happen. Nobody can stop it. Where you going, Daddy?" Giselle asked with a questioning look.

See, that was exactly what I'd been talking about. My daughter was too damn smart for her own good. Even though she knew to stay out of grown people's business, she knew something wasn't right when she heard her daddy was going away. I had made a promise to my daughter long ago that I would never leave her, and I would always be there for her. I'd kill anybody who tried to get in the way of that—brother or not.

"Your uncle is a dumb ass clown," I told her, forgetting who I was talking to for a minute. "He doesn't know what he's talking about, Princess. I'm not going anywhere, and neither are you," I said just as a familiar face walked past my car.

I didn't say anything, because our last encounter ended on a sour note. I would've been lying if I said that I didn't feel some type of way about it because that wasn't how I'd planned for things to go that day. My eyes traveled from the way her ass jiggled in the Nike leggings she had on to the little girl she had trailing by her side that looked to be about Giselle's age.

"Come on, Princess," I said as I hit the locks for us to get out.

Giselle looked as if she wanted to ask a question, but she quickly changed her mind, and I was grateful for that. I didn't have an answer for the shit that I was doing. This girl had me doing shit that was way out of my element since that night at the club.

When we walked in, the two of them were still at the counter ordering, so I walked up.

"I got it," I said just as I saw her reaching into her purse.

She looked at me funny then looked to Giselle before fixing her face. She gave her a little smile before shaking her head at me.

"You don't have to do that. I—"

"I said I got it, ma. Just chill. Tell her I got it, Princess," I used Giselle as my cosigner.

"Yup, Daddy got it! He always got it," she said as I placed the money on the counter.

She let out a little laugh before finally stepping back and letting me do my thing. When the cashier gave me back my change, I kneeled in front of the chocolate cutie she was holding hands with. I could tell this was her daughter because she looked just like her.

"What's your name, cutie?" I asked.

She looked up at her mom, and she nodded, telling her it was okay to tell me, and I couldn't do anything but respect that. She turned back to me and gave me the cutest smile I'd ever seen before answering me.

"Zamani."

"Pretty name for a pretty girl. I'm Boss, and this is Giselle," I introduced.

The girls exchanged their hellos before Zamani introduced me to her mom.

"This my mommy," she said.

"What's her name?" Giselle asked the question I didn't want to ask myself.

"Her name, Mommy," she said, which caused all of us to laugh— even the guy that was fixing their ice cream.

"My name is Choyce, sweetie," she chuckled.

I finally had a name to go with the face and body of the girl who, for some strange reason, I couldn't keep off my mind since we'd crossed paths. The man behind the counter gave Choyce her banana split and Zamani her swirl ice cream cone. Before Zamani could even taste her cone, Choyce was on her ass.

"What do you say to him for buying your ice cream, Mani?" she asked.

"Thank you," she said sweetly.

Choyce said bye to Giselle and quickly turned on her heels without saying a word to me. I had to laugh a little because the whole time we were in there, she never acknowledged my presence.

"Aye, Choyce!" I called after her.

Giselle and Zamani were now engrossed in their own little conversation with each other and paying us no mind. I pulled her off to the side where we were able to talk but still keep our eyes on the girls.

"What?"

"I, uhh, …wanted to apologize for what I said the last time I saw you. I ain't really mean it, and it was basically a figure of speech. As you can see, I'm raising a daughter, so disrespecting women ain't really my thing," I let her know.

"It's cool, Boss. I'm over it." She shrugged it off before trying to take a step around me, but I lightly placed my hand on her waist to stop her.

"I—"

"What do you want from me?" she questioned, throwing me off. "Let me guess, you don't know, but you think I'm bad as hell, and you wanna get to know me?" She rolled her eyes as if niggas had hit her with that weak ass line too many times before.

"I mean, yeah. Ain't no harm in that, right?" I asked.

"As you can see, I have my hands full right now and don't have

48

time for any of the extra shit. If you're serious, I mean *really* serious, about getting to know me as you say, take me out on a date and get to know me. If you're serious, which I highly doubt, you know where to find me," she said before walking off.

I wiped my hands around my mouth as I watched her walk away with her daughter in tow. Giselle slowly walked over to me and grabbed my hand before looking up at me with those honey-colored eyes she'd inherited from me.

"She's pretty, Daddy. I mean, really, really pretty," Giselle informed.

"I know." I smiled as I led her back to the car.

Even long after Choyce was no longer in my presence, she was still heavy on my mind. She talked to me the way no woman besides my mama had talked to me. Hell, Gianna had never talked to me crazy in all the years I had known her. She knew who I was and all about my reputation in the streets, but she acted as if she didn't care about any of that. I think that was what intrigued me the most about her.

Choyce

I was in the locker room, putting the finishing touches on my first outfit of the night when Buffy ran into the room and straight to me.

"Come on, Choyce. We gotta go."

"Uhh, go where?" I asked, dumbfounded.

"A fine ass nigga just promised to pay me two stacks if I find you and bring you to him. Now, stop asking so many questions, and let's go!" Buffy exclaimed.

"Buffy, I—"

"Choyce, don't you start that bullshit with me. You know you are the only bitch in this club that I rock with, so I would never put you in a fucked-up predicament. If I felt like this man was on some bullshit, I never would've even stepped to you about it. That money don't mean shit to me; your safety does. The fact that this man walked in, came straight to me, and the only words out of his mouth were *I got two stacks if you bring Choyce to me* lets me know that he means business," Buffy explained.

I found it kind of odd that whomever this man was had used my real name instead of Hershey, the stage name I gave everybody. At first, I thought it could've been Turelle, but I knew he wouldn't dare be that bold. Besides, he hadn't been seen around the club in a while, and I was grateful for that. No longer putting up a fight, I let Buffy lead me out of the room and out into the club area where it was starting to get packed.

I crinkled my brow in suspicion when Buffy led me over to where the private rooms were. Everybody that worked in this club knew that I didn't do private rooms under any circumstances. Too much bullshit went down in these rooms, which eventually led to a bitch getting fucked back here. That was people's greatest misconception when it came to me and how I made my money or strippers in general. Just because we walked around the club half naked and grinded our asses on niggas didn't make us hoes.

"I already know what you're thinking, but just calm down," Buffy said just as one of the security guards nodded his head at us.

We came to a stop at one of the first rooms, and Buffy stood to the side as she pushed me in room. I looked at her like she was crazy before I turned around to come face to face with none other than Boss. Shaking my head, I fought hard to hide the small smile that wanted to appear.

"Good looking, ma," he said as he reached in his pocket, giving her the money he'd promised her.

Buffy gave me a goofy grin before running out of the room and back to tend to the bar.

"What are you doing here?" I asked.

"You told me where to find you, so here I am. You ready?" he asked a question of his own.

"Ready for what? To go where?"

"I told you clubs ain't really my thing. I got what I came here for, so I'm ready to go. You ready or not?"

Sure, I would've been missing out on money by leaving with Boss right now, but my bills were paid, and I had enough money left over to splurge on my daughter, so what would missing one day hurt? Plus, Boss really brought his ass all the way to the club just to get me, so it was the least I could do.

"I'm ready, just give me a minute to change," I told him. "I'll meet you up front," I let him know before turning around to head back to the locker room.

As I was walking back to the room, I glanced over at Buffy, who must've been watching my every move because her eyes were already on me. She smiled brightly before giving me a thumbs-up and doing a little tweak. I couldn't do anything but laugh at her goofy ass.

Not paying attention to where I was going, I ran smack dab into somebody.

"Ouch, I'm sorry," I said.

"It's okay, Hershey," Melvin, one of the club's regulars, said.

I tried to move around him, but he stepped in my way to stop me. He didn't say anything; he just stood there looking stupid, so I tried to move around him again, but he did the same as he did before by stepping in my way.

"What's up, Melvin? What can I do for you?" I asked impatiently.

"Where you going, Hershey? I'm trying to get a dance," he said through a sniffle as he rubbed his nose.

"Sorry, Melvin. You know I would take care of you, but I'm kind of in a rush right now. Have one of the other girls dance for you," I said as I tried to step around him once again.

"I don't want nobody else," he said as he grabbed my arm tightly. "I been waiting on you all night, so you gon' dance for me. Don't fucking play with me, bitch," he harshly said as he got close to my face.

"Melvin, you better let me the fuck go," I told him calmly through my teeth.

I didn't know whether this nigga was either high, drunk, or both, but he was coming real out of body right now, and I wasn't feeling the shit. His grip on my arm got tighter as I tried to pull away, but before I could say anything, I heard a menacing voice coming from behind me.

"Is there a problem?"

The question was so simple, but his underlying tone was chilling and caused a chill to go down my spine. Melvin must've felt it too because his grip loosened up, but he didn't bother to let go.

"Nah, Boss. Ain't no problem. I'm just talking to this bitc—"

"Muthafucka, let me break it down for you since that coke got yo' geeked up ass too fucked stupid to understand. It's definitely going to be a problem if you don't get yo' fucking hands off some shit that belongs to me, and you damn sure better not come out yo' mouth to disrespect her," he said at the same time I heard a gun cock.

I overlooked the fact that Boss had just called me his because I knew he was trying to help me out right now. Suddenly, Melvin released me and stepped back with his hands in the air in surrender. He had now turned into a coward.

"Come on, Boss, baby, ain't no need for all that shit. You-you know I was just playing. I ain't know that Hershey was yours. You know I would never disrespect you like that. I apologize, Hershey, we good, right?" Melvin asked with sweat now dripping down his face.

"Nah, y'all ain't good, and I better not ever catch you in her fucking face again. As a matter of fact, don't even bring yo' bitch ass within fifty feet of this club," Boss told him.

"O-okay," Melvin stammered as he quickly rushed past us.

For the first time, I turned around and looked at Boss. He didn't have that same sexy look on his face that I was used to seeing. He now sported a deadly look, and I knew that he had just tapped into the street nigga Boss I'd heard so much about.

"Let me hurry up and get yo' ass out of here before you make me kill a muthafucka," he sneered.

I didn't bother to reply as he followed behind me all the way to the locker room so I could change clothes, and we could be out of here.

§

"It's still early as fuck. What you wanna do? Hit the casino or something?" Boss asked once we were seated inside his Range Rover.

I noticed this wasn't the same car he was driving the last time I saw him. I wasn't going to speak on it, though. It was normal for men in his profession to switch cars like they switched their draws ... and women.

"Uhh, I don't think that's a good idea."

"Why not? You got a gambling problem or something?"

"I'm not twenty-one yet," I informed him.

"The fuck?" he said as he looked at me like I was crazy. "How old are you then?"

"I just turned twenty."

"Damn, you really a fucking baby, dude. With a body and ass like that, I never would've known. Don't get me wrong, you do have a baby face, but that ass screams grown woman," he said.

Normally, I would've be offended or shied away from the subject when people talked about my body, but I knew his ass meant no harm.

"Do you always say the first thing that comes to your mind?" I giggled.

"Hell yeah, I'm an honest person. I don't know no other way to be," he shrugged.

"Right," I said as if I didn't believe him.

"Whoa, what the hell is that supposed to mean?" he asked, taking his eyes off the road.

"Keep your eyes on the road!"

"You scared?" he asked as he continued to stare at me while driving.

I tore my eyes away from him and glanced at the dashboard as the speed kept going up. It went from sixty to eighty-five to one hundred. I looked outside the window, and it looked like a bunch of funny lights. With his eyes still on me, Boss just drove as if he had zero fucks to give.

Oh my God, this nigga is really crazy.

Licking his lips, a small, crooked, devilish smile formed on his lips. Finally, I felt the truck slowing down, and I let go of the breath I didn't even know I was holding.

"Yeah, everything you heard about me is true. I'm crazy as fuck," he said as if he could read my mind.

"Don't be doing that; I gotta go home to my daughter." I hit him in his arm, which I was sure didn't faze him.

"Girl, I do too." He laughed before getting serious. "So, where's Zamani's dad?" he asked.

Just thinking about Turelle put me in a bad mood. I didn't have many regrets in life, but he was one of them.

"He has made it very clear on more than one occasion that he wants nothing to do with my daughter, so I don't even bother him. I've been raising her on my own for the past four years. She don't have a daddy," I shrugged.

"I hate niggas like that. They love the action of laying down to make a baby but don't want the responsibility of actually taking care of or raising a baby. That's bitch-nigga shit. I don't want them type of niggas around me," Boss spat.

I wanted to let him know that he already had a nigga like that around him—close to him actually—but I just let it go. I didn't even want people knowing that I was associated with Turelle in any type of way. I'd been doing a good job at it for the past four years, and I would love to keep things the way they were.

"I agree completely. Where's Giselle's mother?" I threw back at him.

"Shit, she don't have a mama. Her trifling ass thought a crack pipe and needle were more important than her only child, so fuck her."

I could tell by the way he said that that it gravely affected him even though he tried to act as if didn't.

"I'm sorry."

"You don't have to apologize for her fuck ups. She's the one missing out on a special little girl. The same goes for Zamani's dad; fuck that nigga. She's probably better off without his ass anyway."

I just nodded my head because he didn't even know the half. I grew up without a father, and you might as well say without a mother too. I always said that if I ever had kids, I didn't want them to grow up like that, but it was funny how life worked. Even though having and raising a child on my own while I was young was hard as hell, I would rather struggle than to beg a soul to help me. Especially Turelle.

Even though I didn't see his true colors until after I found out I was pregnant, I was happy I know what I know now. No, I wasn't perfect, by any means, and I had my faults, but I knew if I ain't shit else, I was a damn good mother, and nobody could tell me differently.

Johann

"*W*alker, how old is that pretty little thing you got back home?" Private Brown asked as he wiped the sweat from his brow with the back of his hand.

"Three years old tomorrow," I smiled brightly.

As if it weren't already hot enough in Afghanistan, we had these hot ass uniforms on, carrying around this heavy ass artillery. It seemed as if no air was being circulated in our vehicle as we rode down the dusty road. Even though the sun was setting, so we had some relief, it was still hot as fuck.

"She sure is gorgeous. I know she had to get her looks from her beautiful mother because she looks nothing like your ugly ass." Brown cracked.

"Man, don't—"

Kaboom!

The vehicle exploding in front of us caused the dark sky to light up at the same time my ears starting ringing from the deadly sound.

"We're being ambushed!"

I could barely make out who was yelling or where the gunfire was coming from, but there was no need. I fully understood what was going on. Due to the explosion, we had been thrown from our vehicle, so I was currently on the ground, scrambling for my gun as our enemies attacked us, and my comrades fought against them.

Kissing my dog tag, I found my firearm and opened fire in the direction our enemies were. Thanks to the night vision goggles that covered my eyes, I could make them out in the dark as I dropped them like flies.

After what seemed like forever, the gunfire had finally ceased. I looked around at all my fallen comrades along with the enemies that didn't make it out alive.

"Shit! Brown!" I yelled as I rushed over to his aid.

He had a pool of blood trailing from his body, coming from the bullet hole in his head. I fought hard to hold back my tears as I used my shaky fingers to close his eyelids. I heard something from behind me and immediately went into defense mode, grabbing my gun and firing it.

"Oh, shit!" I whispered to myself when I realized I had just put three bullets in a child.

"Arghhh!" I yelled out with my gun aimed at something that wasn't even there.

I fought hard to catch my breath and slow my breathing down while lowering my gun. I, as well as my sheets, were now drenched in sweat due to the same nightmare I had been reliving for years.

Fuck this bullshit.

Getting up, I made my way to the bathroom to throw some cold water in my face to help cool me down. I looked in the mirror as the droplets of water ran down my face. I saw nothing but dark, cold eyes that hid a story of pain staring back at me. Dark, cold eyes that belonged to my father. Eyes I hated.

The ringing of my phone caused me to snap out of the trance I had unwillingly let myself get into. I snatched a towel off the rack and quickly dried my face to see who the hell was calling me at damn near five in the morning.

Seeing that it was my mom, I rushed to answer it.

"What's wrong, Mama?" I questioned.

"You had another one; I can feel it," she said with her voice laced with worry.

Sighing, I tugged at the hairs in my thick beard. "Mama, go back to sleep. I'm fine," I told her.

"Hanny."

"Yes, Mama?" I asked, sounding like a child, but my mama had that type of effect on me.

"Have you been going to the therapist?" she questioned.

I groaned in agony at the fact that she brought that bullshit up. The fuck did I look like going to see a fucking quack who, nine times outta ten, wasn't right in his fucking head either? That shit wasn't for me, and I ain't need it.

"No," I told her flat out. "I'm good. ... I'm doing better. I'll be alright," I let her know.

Being diagnosed with PTSD was common for a soldier when they came home from the war. The shit you saw while in combat would fuck with your mental and turn you into a completely different person. One thing about it, though—I was dealing with this shit on my own. I ain't need anybody to tell me that I was fucking crazy. I was sane as hell; all the rest of you muthafuckas are the crazy ones.

The line went quiet for a while before my mama spoke again. "Romans 15:13. I love you, Johann," she said softly.

"I love you, too," I said just above a whisper before the call was disconnected.

After taking a quick shower and changing my sheets, I reached in the drawer of my nightstand and pulled out the Bible I kept in there. I went straight to the Bible verse my mama quoted and began to read it. I highlighted it like I did all the other verses she told me to read whenever I had one of those punk ass nightmares.

Feeling a sense of peace, I laid back down to try to get some shuteye for at least another hour or two.

§

Walking into the warehouse that Boss and I used for our own little gun range, I found this nigga sitting in the middle of the room with his feet up while he was slouched down in the chair, grinning from ear to ear. He was so engrossed in his conversation that he ain't even notice I was there.

"Fuck you grinning so hard for, bitch?" I questioned while I slapped him in the back of his head.

Boss jumped and reached for the gun that he had laying on the table but slowly sat back when he noticed who I was.

"I'ma call you back," he said into the phone. "Man, you better stop fucking playing with me and answer when I call you back," he said with a smile on his face.

I stood there with my face scrunched up as I saw a foreign ass side of my right-hand man that I hadn't seen in years. The only person I knew that could make his ass smile this much was my god baby, and I could tell just by his end of the conversation that it definitely wasn't her on the other of the phone.

"You's a bitch," Boss threw at me once he ended his phone call.

"I'm the bitch?" I pointed at myself. "How, when you the one sitting there with the fucking heart eyes and little pink hearts floating all around yo' damn head and shit?" I cracked.

"Get the fuck outta here. Never." He waved me off.

"Nah, on some real shit, though. What the hell you got going on? Who was that?" I asked as I sat at the table he was sitting at.

"Choyce," he said. He must've realized I ain't know who the fuck that was, so he went ahead and elaborated for me. "Ol' girl from the club that night."

A big ass grin formed on my face when I remembered who he was talking about. I knew he had run into her a few times since that, but I didn't know shit had gotten that far between them. Hell, I knew I told him he'd better get her name the next time he saw her, but Boss was a different type of nigga. He didn't allow any bitch to get close to him, so the fact that he was even sitting here holding a conversation with her over the phone was crazy.

"Damn, so my nigga coming out of retirement?" I asked for

CHARMANIE SAQUEA

clarification.

"Nah, nah, it ain't nothing like that. She got a daughter that's a year younger than Giselle, so we was setting up a play date." He shrugged as if it weren't shit.

"So you about to be playing stepdaddy now? She may be fine and all that, but ain't no bitch worth all that baby daddy drama shit," I let him know.

"Come on, man, chill out. The only thing you need to be worried about is finding somebody for yo' crazy ass to settle down with. It's been long enough, bro," Boss stated.

I shook my head in the negative. I couldn't even see myself finding a bitch that could hold my attention long enough for me to like her ass—let alone trying to settle down with one. I honestly didn't even think that shit was in the cards for me. I was good with just fucking bitches and moving on to the next. That way, I ain't have to commit to one. At the end of the day, we both got something out of it—a good ole nut.

Fuck all that extra shit.

Relationships weren't for me, and I wasn't about to try and make them for me.

"My bad, Han. I ain't mean—"

"Nigga, let me see if that aim still on point since you ain't out here laying niggas down like you used to. I think yo' ass done got too comfortable out here," I cut him off while cocking my gun after making sure the clip was full.

63

"Never comfortable, baby. Plus, I ain't out here laying niggas down, because muthafuckas is out here acting like they got some damn sense. If a nigga ever forgets who the fuck I am and try to come at me crazy, his ass gon' get hit with these hollow tips," Boss said with a crooked smirk as he walked over and lined up with his target.

Following suit, I walked over to my target, and Boss gave the signal for us to start. Seconds later, the warehouse erupted in gunfire. After we emptied our clips, we walked closer to our targets to see how we did.

"And niggas think I'm slipping on this gunplay shit. Straight headshots with two to the heart," Boss bragged.

"You better stay on yo' a-game nigga. You never know when a nigga gon' start feeling beside himself and try to come at you," I let him know.

"Yup, and his ass gon' end up just like this," he said as he held up his paper target that was full of bullet holes.

I just laughed at his crazy ass. People always thought I was the crazier one out of the two of us, but if only they knew. Unlike me, Boss learned how to contain his shit until it was necessary to let the beast out. There was a completely different side to that nigga that nobody ever wanted to meet.

Boss

$\mathcal{S}$tepping out of the car, I hit the locks as I glanced at the time on my Rolex. As I made my way into the building, I instantly caught a bad feeling. Just to know that I was surrounded by so many pigs made me sick, but the fact that a nigga I shared the same blood with was actually one of those pigs made me repulsed.

Instantly, my eyes locked on his bitch ass, and I made my way over to him. Hendrix looked up at me as if he were shocked to see me in the station, but he shouldn't have been. He knew what type of nigga I was, so he should've known I gave negative number of fucks.

Slamming his door, I walked over to him and jacked his bitch ass up before he could even get a word out.

"Bitch, you better watch what the fuck you say and do when my fucking daughter is around. If you ever discuss Gianna or her condition with Giselle again, I'll fucking kill you," I said with nothing but venom dripping from each word I spoke.

I didn't know why his ass wanted to try me. He knew better than anybody that I didn't play when it came to my child. The fact that he felt so comfortable or compelled to tell Giselle that her mama was a crackhead or that I sold drugs was beyond me. My daughter was innocent when it came to every situation that went on around her. If

I wanted her to know Gianna wasn't in her life because she was on drugs, then I would've told her that shit myself.

I wasn't the type to keep anything away from Giselle. I always tried my best to answer her questions when she asked them, no matter how off the wall they might've been. Some shit, though, I would rather explain to her when she got older and was able to understand better.

"Boston, if I were you, I would release the hold you have on me, or—"

"Or you'll do what, pussy? You know I don't take kindly to threats," I warned his ass.

Hendrix clenched his jaws, but he didn't bother to speak another word. He knew he couldn't handle me, big brother or not. I wished his little square ass would just stop trying to act like he was hard or something. To these muthafuckas around the police station or common criminals, he might've been the big kahuna, but to me and all the rest of the people who knew him—the real him—he was soft as fucking cotton.

Finally letting him go and stepping back, I gave his ass an ice grill that was cold enough to freeze hell over. Every time I looked at the nigga that I shared the same parents with, I wanted to beat his ass. I didn't know why I was surprised when he crossed me by going behind my back and fucking Gianna. I should've expected the shit.

Ever since we were kids, my brother had been in competition with me, and the shit was dumb as hell. There wasn't shit I wouldn't have done for Hendrix even when I knew he couldn't stand me. That was just the type of nigga that I was and how deep my loyalty ran until you did some snake shit and crossed me, and that was exactly what he had done.

"It's been years, Boss. Let that shit go. I ain't force Gianna to do shit she ain't wanna do. You claim you don't want her no more, but every time you see your *brother,* you come at me sideways over a bitch you knew wasn't shit from the jump," Hendrix had the audacity to tell me.

I couldn't help myself. I had no choice but to scoff at the fact that he had the nerve to put emphasis on the word brother like that meant something to him.

Ol' clown ass nigga.

"Stop fucking testing me, Hendrix, before I give you what you want, and you gonna wish you had never brought that side of me back out. The only thing keeping me off yo' ass is that I know it'll break my mama's heart for her to know her youngest son is responsible for killing her oldest," I told him honestly.

He just didn't know the love and respect I had for our mama was the only reason I hadn't handled his ass yet. I hadn't even beat his ass for the bullshit he did to me just for the simple fact that my mama raised us better than that. Soon, and very soon, though, Hendrix was going to find himself in a fucked-up situation that not even my mama could save him from.

"You're pretty bold, coming down here and threatening me, knowing what I'm capable of doing to you."

"Bitch, you not gon' do shit!" I sneered as I walked up to him again. "If you wanted to fuck with me, yo' soft ass would've did it years ago. You's a bitch. and the only thing you're capable of doing is getting yo' ass fucked over fucking with me. Keep. Fucking. Trying. Me." I gave him one final warning before walking out of his office just as smoothly as I'd come in.

For years, I tried to make amends with Hendrix even though I wasn't the reason we were at odds with each other in the first place. At this point, I was over him and all his bullshit. Any other nigga would've killed his ass for fucking their bitch, but I left the shit alone because, at the end of the day, we were brothers whether either of us liked it or not. Now, I was ready to wash my hands of his ass, but that was not what Hendrix wanted me to do. He should've been trying to stay on my good side instead of trying to have me as an enemy.

My pops always said to watch those closest to you because they might be the reason for your demise one day. I never thought he would be speaking of his own son.

Damn.

§

Cruising through the streets of Detroit, I couldn't help but reminisce on how things used to be. I came a long way from the bad ass little nigga who used to fight all the older boys in the area of 7 Mile and Evergreen. From running errands for the local hustlers to eventually sneaking around and selling with them. That was how I got put on.

One day, my mama was washing my clothes when she went into my closet to hang something up. She found some weed that I didn't hide all the way. She told my pops, and he was literally waiting for my ass at the door when I came home. I thought it was going to be a wrap for my ass, but I got the shock of my life.

He looked me dead in my eyes and told me nobody was going to teach his son the game better than he could. He told me he couldn't even be mad at me, because he knew the shit was inevitable. He had never hidden his past or past transgressions from us, so we knew he used to be heavy in the streets until he finally decided to retire.

That day was the day that my pops started grooming my right-hand man, Han, and me for the streets. Han's home life was a little fucked up even though he didn't like speaking on it, so my pops stepped in to play the father role for him. We went from selling petty ass weed to moving work in a matter of no time. Of course, that caused some tension between us and the niggas that were already established, but they soon found out we weren't to be fucked with.

Those were the good days.

Now, shit was so fucked up that it made no sense. Whoever said more money meant more problems never lied. These days, you had niggas you grew up with from the sandbox and even your own family ready to put a bullet in the back of your head all in the name of a dollar or just because they were envious. Shit was just ridiculous. I didn't know who was raising these pussy ass niggas, because they were certainly a different breed.

My ringing phone cut my reminiscing session short. With a smile, I rushed to answer it.

"What's up, baby girl?" I answered.

"Boston, guess what's coming up!"

"Damn, I hope not the first, because I don't feel like paying no bills," I half joked.

"You're such an asshole, but that's cool because you won't have to pay them anymore. At least not here, because I'm coming home!" Freedom squealed with excitement.

I pulled the phone away from my ear and looked at it like it was contaminated or something because she had me fucked up. Freedom was my daughter before I fucked around and had my own child. Being that she was my baby sister and the youngest of the three of us, she was spoiled rotten. When she was in her senior year of high school, we made a deal that I would send her to any school she wanted to attend, and all she had to do was get nothing less than a C and graduate, and she wouldn't have to worry about paying for shit. That included her tuition and whatever other bills she had. She had been holding up her end of the deal, so it was only right that I held up my end as well.

"No the fuck you not. Where you get that bullshit from?" I questioned.

When I sent Freedom away, it was mainly to get her the fuck away from Detroit so she could do something with her life. She had always been a good girl with a good head on her shoulders, and I didn't want her getting caught up with one of these no-good ass niggas around here and throwing all that shit away.

"Boss," she whined. "That's not fair. I graduate in a few weeks, and I'm ready to come home. I miss you, and I miss Mommy. Even though she won't tell me, and you'll lie to keep me here, I know she's not doing good right now, and I just want to be around her," Freedom continued to whine.

"Dom, you know how I feel about you being here," I told her.

"I know, Boss. Just let me come until school starts back up in a few months. Then, I'll come back. I promise. You're coming down here for my graduation, right?" she asked me a dumb ass question.

"Girl, don't fucking play with me. You know damn well I'ma be there."

"Okay, so I'll start packing because I'm coming back home with you. Love you, Boss! See you in about two weeks!" she said quickly before hanging up so I wouldn't protest.

I just shook my head because I should've known I was fighting a losing battle. I was far from a sucka ass nigga, but it seemed as if the women in my life always seemed to get their way when it came to me, no matter how much I tried to put my foot down—from my Mama to my sister and now my daughter. I couldn't blame nobody but myself, though, because I had them like that.

That's exactly why I'm single now.

I tried to do the same thing for a bitch, once upon a time, but she didn't appreciate the shit I did for her. After Gianna's trifling ass, I vowed to never give a female that didn't share the same blood as me my all, and I meant that. So far, so good.

Choyce

*B*rushing my hair into a high bun on the top of my head, I looked over myself once more, trying to figure out whether this was what I really wanted to wear.

"If I didn't know any better, I would think yo' ass is the one going on a date, not Mani," Jamaica said from the doorway. "Let me find out you tryna *boss* your life up," she cracked, trying to be funny by emphasizing the word boss.

Boss had hit me up with the idea of Giselle and Zamani having a play date, and I didn't see anything wrong with that. I thought it would be good for Zamani to interact with another child that was around her age. Since she was the only child, wasn't in school yet, and I wasn't close to my family, she didn't have any other kids to hang around or play with. I knew she was tired of being around me all day, every day, so I was happy he'd suggested it.

"Ha-ha, I see you got jokes. I'm not even thinking about that man. Don't get me wrong, he's cool and all that, but I'm not interested," I let her know.

"Tuh, you need to be interested or at least get you some di—"

"Mani, you ready?" I cut Jamaica's wild ass off.

Everybody had that one friend that had no filter, and Jamaica was definitely that friend. She never stopped to think before she spoke, therefore she always said the first thing that was on her mind. Of course, it got her into more trouble than it should have, but she wasn't the type to ever give a fuck. Jamaica was the definition of 'crazy as hell,' but that was my baby, and I didn't know what I would do without her.

"Don't be trying to cut me off. Mommy needs a boyfriend, ain't that right, Zamani?" Jamaica asked with a devilish smile on her face.

"Uhn hun," my baby said even though she ain't even know what she was cosigning on.

She was too busy with her head deep into her tablet to even care about what we were talking about. All she did was sit on that damn tablet on YouTube, watching other kids play games. I thought the shit was stupid, but whatever held her attention and kept her off my nerves was good to me.

"Come on, baby. Let's go so you can have fun," I told her while taking the tablet from her and plugging it into the charger.

"Have fun, ladies. I'll be here when you two get back so you can tell me all about it," Jamaica said as she walked us to the door.

I just cut my eyes at her as I carried Zamani out to the car and strapped her into her car seat. Every time I looked at my daughter, my heart just swelled up with joy and pride. Even though Zamani was conceived under some fucked up circumstances, and I wished that I had waited until I was older and ready before having a baby, I wouldn't trade her for anything in this world.

She meant the world to me, and I couldn't imagine my life without her. The past four years of my life with her, I'd been the happiest I'd ever been in life.

"I love you," I told her before giving her a kiss.

"Love you, Mommy!" she said, full of excitement.

After making sure Zamani was secure, I hopped in the driver's seat and peeled out of the driveway. I played my baby's favorite song that she just insisted on hearing every time she was in the car. As soon as 'That's What I Like' by Bruno Mars came through the speakers, I glanced in my rearview mirror just as she started dancing in her seat.

"Lucky for you, that's what I like. That's what I like," the both of us sang along with Bruno as I cruised through the streets of Detroit.

After some time, we had finally reached our destination, in Troy. Pulling out my phone, I called up Boss to see if he had made it yet.

"Yo," he answered.

"What I tell you about that?" I asked.

Boss answered the phone all types of ways except how he should've. I told him before that I was not one of his homeboys, so he needed to answer my calls like he had some sense.

"My bad," he chuckled. "I mean hello?" he corrected himself.

"That's better, but I was just calling to let you know that we just pulled up," I let him know.

"Coo', come in. We'll meet you at the door," he said.

After disconnecting the call, I got Zamani out of the car so we could go in. Just as he said they would, Boss and Giselle were waiting for us when we walked in.

"Zamani! Miss Choyce!" Giselle's lil' cute self said as she took off running for us.

She and Zamani hugged each other as if they were best friends that hadn't seen each other in years. I thought the sight was just the cutest thing ever. I loved how excited they were to see each other.

"You ain't have no trouble getting here, did you?" Boss inquired as he pulled me into his strong arms for a hug.

I was instantly captivated by his cologne. Not only did this man look and dress good, but he always smelled good as hell. That was a bonus in my book. Besides at the club, it had been years since I'd last felt a man's touch, and I would've been lying if I said that it didn't feel good as hell to be wrapped up in his arms. The way he firmly held me as his hands rested just at the top of my ass felt so good but foreign at the same time.

"Nope, no trouble at all. You look cute, though," I complimented him once we pulled back from our hug.

Licking his lips, Boss gave me a crooked smile while rubbing his hands together slowly.

"Just cute, huh? Here I was, thinking I was sexy as hell, and you hurting my feelings with this cute shit like I'm a lil' nigga or something."

Even though I could tell that he was joking, I still sensed some sincerity in his words. Boss was so used to women salivating over him everywhere he went that he didn't know how to feel when he wasn't receiving that type of attention. I found it to be quite comical.

"If you don't cut it out," I playfully rolled my eyes at him.

"Miss Choyce, can we play now? Please?" Giselle asked.

"Please, Mommy?" Zamani followed suit.

I let out a little laugh at the fact that Giselle was really calling me Miss. I was only twenty years old and had never been called that before.

"Let me pay for Zamani—"

"Aye, don't insult me like that," Boss cut me off.

"What happened? What I do?" I questioned, truly confused.

"Everything already taken care of. Let the little rugrats go have some fun. Just make sure y'all stay where we can see you," Boss instructed them.

It was as if that was all the girls needed to hear before they took off. Hand in hand, they ran off together with neither Boss nor me on their minds.

"Thank you for inviting Mani to come have some fun. She doesn't really get to do things like this," I thanked Boss.

"It's no problem. Giselle was ready to kick my ass if she didn't get to see her new friend. But what's been up with you, Miss Choyce?" Boss asked with a smile as we found ourselves a table to sit at so we could watch the girls.

"Nothing much," I sighed. "Just trying to finish this school shit so I can finally get my ass out the strip club," I told him honestly.

Even though the money I made stripping was good as hell and enough to support Zamani and I, I was ready for something different. The club was just supposed to be something to do for me at that moment, but somewhere along the lines, I kind of let that lifestyle suck me in. I had dreams, goals, and aspirations in life that I wanted to achieve, but I couldn't do any of that without my high school diploma and a degree.

"So, you in school? Where you go? To Wayne?" Boss inquired.

"Don't judge me, but I'm taking classes to get my GED. I got pregnant with Mani when I was fifteen and had her when I was sixteen. I had zero support from my family and, of course, her dad, so I dropped out of high school my junior year," I explained.

"Why would I judge you for that?" he asked with his face screwed up. "Listen, baby, ain't shit wrong with wanting to better yourself. At least you want better and taking the initiative to make shit shake. A lot of bitches would've just used their circumstances as an excuse and be looking for handouts for the rest of their lives. You got ambition and a good head on your shoulders; I like that shit."

I don't know why, but for some reason, him saying that made me feel good. Not a lot of people had positive things to say about me, but to hear someone who barely knew me compliment me like that made me proud.

"Thank you," I smiled.

"You're welcome. So, after you get your GED, what you gonna do? You gonna enroll in college? I know I'm all up in ya business and shit, but a nigga just tryna get to know you," he said as he ran his thick ass pink tongue over his sexy ass lips.

Damn, this man is fine.

"No, it's fine. I don't really share this type of stuff with people, so it feels good to actually talk about it with someone. I want to go to college and get a degree in business management or something. I want to open up my own little spa that's strictly dedicated to kids. Little girls can come for like their birthday and get catered to. They can get little manis and pedis, little massages, and facials. The whole nine yards," I beamed as I talked about it.

Basically, my whole life, I grew up with low self-esteem from being talked about because I was darker than everyone else. Nobody ever made me feel good about myself or spoke life into me to let me know that I was beautiful in the skin I was in. I swore that if I ever had kids, I would let them know every day that they were made to perfection and didn't have a single flaw.

Every day, I tried to uplift my baby and instill the confidence in her that I never had. The smile that she had on her face whenever I did her hair or painted her nails was something that I cherished deeply. Now, I wanted to see that smile on other little girl's faces; that was why I wanted to open my own spa for them—so they could feel and know that they were beautiful all the time.

"What?" I nervously asked Boss because he was looking at me funny.

"That shit is dope, Choyce. I ain't never heard of no shit like that, but it's a good ass idea. Giselle is a fucking diva already, so I know she'll love to go to a spot like that. Hell yeah, that's dope, baby. Make it happen. I can already tell that shit gon' be a success," Boss told me.

"You just saying that." I waved him off.

"What? Girl, you should know by now that I have zero problems saying how I feel. If I thought the shit was wack, I would've said so. Think about how many kids get tired of doing the same ol' bullshit for their birthdays. Sick of going to some damn Chuck E. Cheese. The shit you wanna do for the kids is different, and the parents of daughters would love that for their girls and her friends," he explained.

"Yeah, you're right. I thought it sounded crazy, so I never told anybody what I wanted to do," I shrugged.

"So why you tell me then?" Boss questioned, throwing me off as he got closer to me.

"I-I don't know. You. ... I just feel comfortable around you, I guess," I stammered.

Some way, somehow, his hand had found its way to my thigh. The way his hand was stroking my thigh was causing my thoughts to become a little cloudy, and I couldn't think. I quickly scanned the area to make sure the girls or anyone else, for that matter, weren't paying attention to what he was doing.

"You so sexy; you know that, right?" he asked softly as his hands found their way up the dress I had on. "You knew what the fuck you was doing by wearing this, huh? You was tryna get my attention, Choyce?" he asked as he brushed his fingers across my thong.

I was now starting to regret wearing this dress. Never would I have thought that Boss would be in here—a kid's establishment—running his fingers across my southern pair of lips. Even though he had done it the same the night I met him in the club, this was completely different and wild.

"The kids, Boss," I reminded him as I tried to clench my legs together to stop him.

"They don't give a fuck about shit we got going on right now. Open up," he said in a gentle yet demanding tone.

Looking around nervously, I tried to push his hand away on the sly, but Boss wasn't having that. He grabbed the thin fabric in the middle of my thong and yanked it, causing it to rip. I let out a gasp just as his fingers found their way in my entrance.

"Damn, you wet ... and tight," Boss whispered as he probed his fingers around.

I had to bite my lip to keep from letting out the loudest moan ever. I was embarrassed to say, but I'd had no sexual activity in my life since before Zamani was born. I had never let another man get close to me since Turelle and I broke up. Now, here I was, getting my pussy played with, and my daughter wasn't even fifty feet away. If I were light skinned, I would've definitely been red right now.

"Uhh," I accidentally let slip out.

"Shhh," Boss whispered in my ear as he moved his fingers as if he were beckoning me to come here.

I couldn't take it anymore; my stomach felt as if it were getting tight, and the pressure that was building up was becoming too much for me. I tried to fight it, but it felt as if I were losing the battle.

"Let that shit go," Boss demanded as he moved his fingers faster.

Suddenly, it seemed as if I couldn't control my body as I started shaking while I felt myself raining down. Embarrassed, I placed my head in my hands as Boss finally removed his fingers. I peeked at him through the cracks of my fingers, and his nasty ass had the nerve to stick his fingers in his mouth.

"Sweet, just like I knew you would be," he smirked. "You good?" he asked through a chuckle.

"I ... I'll be back," I quickly said before getting up as fast as my legs would allow me to.

I rushed to the bathroom and into the nearest stall I could get to. I was thankful I carried feminine wipes around with me even though I never thought I would need them for some shit like this. Being a stripper, it just kinda came natural to me. As I was cleaning myself off, I really thought about what had just taken place. I had never done any shit like that before. Although I'd only been with one man, Turelle was never that freaky. Boss was just on another level when it came to everything.

I see why he's the Boss.

Turk

I lightly tapped on the door before entering. Boss had sent for me because he claimed he had something he needed to speak with me about. If it wasn't about getting me out the trap house and back on the streets, being a lieutenant like I was supposed to be, then I wasn't tryna hear shit he had to say. He had his phone glued to his ear with his feet up on the desk.

"I'm not doing shit tonight but working unless I get to see you," he said into the phone.

Ol' cupcake ass nigga.

For somebody who claimed they needed to speak with me, his ass was making no effort to end his conversation. His soft ass would rather be in here caked up with a bitch instead of handling business like he was supposed to. That was what was wrong with his little fruit ass now. Him and his bitch ass boyfriend—Han. Couldn't nobody tell me them niggas weren't fucking each other in the ass. Ain't no way in hell two niggas were that close without being butt buddies. The shit just wasn't realistic.

"Nah, not there," he said into the phone before pausing. "C'mon, baby, you know I don't like being in them type of environments. I'm not no regular ass nigga, so I can't do no regular ass shit," he said.

I let out a little laugh at that one as I adjusted the way I was sitting in my seat. I was starting to become impatient with this shit, and I wanted him to know. Boss cut his eyes at me, but I ignored his ass.

Finally, after about another twenty minutes, he decided that he wanted to get off the phone. He took his feet off his desk and sat up in his seat before leaning on his forearms as he crossed his hands together.

"You got somewhere you need to be or something?" he asked with more attitude than he needed to.

"Nah, why you ask that?"

"Nigga, I done told you about answering me what that 'nah' bullshit. I'm not with all that ignorant shit. Answer me like you got some damn sense. Anyway, you in here huffing and puffing like you got someplace other than here to be."

"I mean, you did ask me to take this trip all the way out here because you had to talk to me, but you all on the phone," I told him.

I didn't know why his pretty boy ass thought somebody was supposed to be scared of him. He might've been 'that nigga' or ruthless to everybody else, but he was pussy to me. If I hadn't been making good money with his ass, I would've been got the fuck on. It was cool, though, because I had a plan already in motion. I was just waiting for the perfect time to execute it.

"And? You on my time. I'm not on yours, so if I wanted to continue on with my conversation for another hour, then I could've. You don't run shit but yo' damn mouth around here, Turk. That's why yo' ass always in some fucked up shit. Learn to shut the fuck up sometimes, nigga," Boss raised his voice.

"Alright," I said as calmly as I could.

He was starting to piss me off, and I ain't feel like rumbling with his ass today. I was still recovering from my gunshot wounds; I ain't have time to be fighting his ass.

"Since you wanted to play the dumb ass role like you ain't know who the fuck would want ya ass dead, I took the initiative to find out my damn self. Come to find out, you got a problem with keeping yo' fucking hands to yo'self. Fuck is you doing putting yo' damn hands on females for?" Boss questioned with a fucked up look on his face.

This nigga couldn't sit up here and question or judge me about the shit I did when I knew he had to slap Gianna's slut ass around before. This nigga was a fucking hypocrite.

"Mannn, it—"

"Man, what? It what? I'm not tryna hear none of that shit right now, Turelle! You fucked around and did some hoe ass shit that damn near made us go into an unnecessary ass street war! You out here tryna test people's hoe card, not even realizing that it's some muthafucka out here that's badder than you and actually live for that gunplay shit. Do you know what happens when we're at war? We don't make money. You know what happens when we don't make money? I get pissed the fuck off because I'm not about to let nobody fuck with my cash flow. Lucky for yo' stupid ass, I was able to have a sit down with them niggas and get everything straightened out because they still want yo' fucking head, but for right now, you good. But since you wanted to lie about yo' shit, I'm extending your probation. I don't even want yo' ass in my traps for ninety days. The only thing you are allowed to sell is weed, and

I'm not paying you until you're off probation. If I were you, I wouldn't fuck up not one time in the next ninety days, because the next step is cutting yo' ass off for good. Now get the fuck outta my face; I'm tired of looking at you."

I sat there in that seat, boiling like a pot of water. If Boss thought he had me fucked up before, he really had me fucked up now. This nigga was on some bullshit, and I just couldn't get jiggy with it. The fuck he mean, I'm not getting paid? Then, he tells me I'm only allowed to sell weed. What type of dope was he smoking? Because he had to have been on drugs to tell me some shit like that.

"You got a fucking problem or something?" he asked once I didn't leave when he called himself dismissing me.

"I feel like you going to the extreme right now, and it don't take all that. For you to say I'm not getting paid for three months is some bullshit," I expressed myself.

"No, what's some bullshit is you being a bitch and hitting a female in her face because you don't like what the fuck she said to yo' dumb ass. Then, for you to sit up in my face and lie when I asked you did you have any idea on who wanted you dead, that's some bullshit. Now, I'm not going to tell you again. … The door."

I ain't like the way this nigga called himself tryna play me, but I let the shit go. Sucking my teeth, I got up from my chair and walked out of his office.

Bitch ass nigga.

Fuck that nigga. He acted as if he were God's gift to the world or something. I couldn't stand niggas who acted invincible.

§

After the bullshit with Boss, I needed something to get my mind off everything, so I hit up my favorite strip club. It was nothing but bad bitches all up and through this bitch. I threw back my shot of patron just as the DJ announced who was coming to the stage next. Suddenly, every nigga in the building started going crazy and pulling stacks and bankrolls out as they moved closer to the stage. I slouched down in my seat just as she made her way.

My eyes zeroed in on Choyce, or Hershey as she went by in the club, as her thick ass moved to the beat of the song. The stage name Hershey was so fitting for her as her chocolate skin glowed under the florescent lights in the club. 'Private Room' by Tony Michael crooned through the speakers as Choyce moved her body, putting every nigga in the building, including me, in a trance.

As I watched her, it was crazy to me that this was the same girl that used to have me gone over her little young ass. I hated to admit it, but there wasn't shit in this world that I wouldn't have done for Choyce, but her dumb ass had to go and fuck all that up. Now, the love I once had in my heart for her was replaced with a deeply seeded hatred.

I couldn't stand her ass now, and every chance I got, I let her know how I felt about her. That bitch tried to play it crazy, talking about I was her baby daddy; that bitch was straight delusional. When she first came at me with that pregnant shit, I told her ass to get a fucking abortion, but she refused, so now, she was raising her child on her own.

At the end of the day, though, I couldn't even lie; the bitch was bad as fuck—always had been. She stood about five foot two with smooth, chocolate skin that was flawless as hell. Her body had developed way before its time, so she was blessed with a set of baby-making hips and an ass that bitches went to Dr. Miami to get. Even after having a baby, her stomach was flat, and her waist was nonexistent. She had a pretty set of big, doe eyes that gave her an innocent look with some sexy ass juicy lips that I knew for a fact were soft as hell.

I couldn't help but lick my lips at the way she did her thing as she climbed all the way up a pole and hit the splits on the ceiling. That was some shit I had never seen before, and sure enough, all the niggas went crazy, flooding the stage with money.

"Damn, that shit is wild as fuck!" I heard a familiar voice say near me.

Cutting my eyes to the side, I noticed Han and Boss were now in attendance. I thought that shit was weird as fuck because Boss never went out to clubs, but now, here he was, staring at Choyce with the fucking googly eyes.

Boss let out a whistle and shook his head as he made his way to the stage. I watched with a raised brow as Choyce crawled over to him once she made her way back down the pole. He whispered something in her ear that caused her to have a smile that was a mile long before she turned around and squatted in front of him, twerking each of her ass cheeks, one at a time. Suddenly, Boss pulled a stack of bills out of nowhere and literally made it storm on Choyce.

I shifted in my seat and sat up a little as I continued to watch the two of them. It was something about their little exchange that I wasn't feeling. That ain't look like a nigga that she ain't know just coming in here and throwing money at her. Nah, the two of them looked too fucking familiar, and I wasn't feeling the shit.

After her set was done, a guard walked out to help Choyce collect her money, and Boss suddenly disappeared. I cut my eyes back over to Han's bitch ass as he stood there, looking stupid while whispering something in one of the other stripper's ears. His pussy hungry ass was always trying to talk a bitch out her drawers. One day, his dumb ass was going to catch something he couldn't get rid of.

Just as I was getting up to go find me a bitch to suck my dick, Choyce and Boss were walking in Han's direction. Together. Hand in hand. I had a deep frown on my face as I watched the bullshit before me. Choyce was now dressed in some leggings and a tight-fitting shirt with her bag tucked under her arm.

"Alright, nigga, we out," Boss told Han.

Choyce must've felt my eyes burning a hole into her because we locked eyes with each other. The smile that was once on her face slowly faded away. I didn't know exactly what the fuck was going on between the two of them, but I was definitely going to find out. Boss said something to Choyce, but she ain't respond right away, because we were still having an intense staring battle. Boss' eyes traveled over to me, and he put a cocky little smirk on his face before pulling her closer to him and leading her out the door.

Dumb ass hoe.

Seeing that just further validated what I already knew about Choyce; she was a hoe and not to be trusted.

Boss

*H*olding my princess in my arms, I made my way up to the address I was given. Before I could even reach the door, it came open, and out stepped Choyce. She had her hair in a messy bun on the top of her head, glasses on, a tank top, and some shorts that had her thick ass thighs on display.

"Sorry it's late, but I ain't have nowhere else to take her," I told Choyce as a very sleepy Giselle lifted her head up to peek at her.

"No need to apologize; just go check on your mom. I hope she feels better," Choyce said softly.

"Thank you. You want me to come and lay her down?" I asked.

Giselle was being a little diva and acting as if she were too sleepy to walk right now. It was almost three o'clock in the morning, and I had woken her up out of her sleep because my mom had to be rushed to the hospital. Han was out somewhere, laid up with only God knows who, so I couldn't take her to her god-daddy. A thought had popped into my head, and I really didn't know whether Choyce was available, because it was Saturday, and I knew, most likely, she would've been at the club. When I called her, she immediately told me to bring Giselle over.

"Yeah, you can lay her down in Mani's room. Her little bad butt decided she was sleeping in my bed tonight," she said as she led me into the house.

As soon as I crossed over the threshold, I felt a sense of calmness that I usually only felt whenever I went to my mama's house. Choyce had her place decked out. Everything in her living room was decorated in earth tones. She had a big ass TV mounted on her wall that curved.

As she led me up the stairs, I couldn't help but keep my eyes glued to her round, juicy ass as it swayed to the beat of its own drum.

"Here we are," Choyce said as she opened the door to the room.

The room was decorated in pinks and purples with a princess theme to it. Zamani was definitely sleeping in style with the little princess bed to match her room. I knew for a fact Giselle was going to love waking up in this room. I laid Sleeping Beauty in the bed and took her shoes off before placing a kiss on her forehead.

"I love you, Princess," I told her.

She mumbled something back that was inaudible, but I knew it was along the lines of I love you too. Walking out of the room, I once again followed behind Choyce as she led the way back down the stairs.

"Thank you so much," I told her once we reached the door. I went in my pocket and pulled out some money to pay her, but she started shaking her head.

"What you doing?" she questioned.

"I know you missing out on money because of me and my inconvenience. I'm compensating you. How much I owe you?"

"Absolutely nothing. Giselle is not an inconvenience, Boss. Just go see about your mom, and text or call me to let me know how she's doing," she said.

I pulled her into a hug and damn near didn't want to let her go because she felt so good and soft. Little did she know—I was going to give her something for looking out for me. I tried to place a kiss on her cheek, but she moved her head too quick, and it landed on the corner of her mouth.

I'm sorry," she said, full of embarrassment as she pulled back from me.

Biting my lip, I grabbed the waistband of her shorts and pulled her back to me, kissing her soft ass lips.

"I'll be back, aight?"

"Okay," Choyce said softly.

Letting my eyes roam over her one final time, I turned on my heels to head to my car. I really hated to leave my princess, but there was no telling how long I was going to be at this hospital, and I wanted her to get some sleep. There weren't many that I trusted with my daughter, but I knew I had nothing to worry about when it came to Choyce. I knew she wouldn't let any harm come Giselle's way.

Twenty minutes later, I was walking through the doors of the emergency room. Walking up to the desk, I asked her to point me in the right direction. I gave her my mama's name, and in return, she gave me her room number. Thanking her, I quickly rushed to the back to see what was wrong with my baby.

When I walked into her room, I ignored Hendrix's bitch ass and went straight to her bed. I ain't like how she was looking or the fact that she was hooked up to an IV and oxygen.

"Hey, baby," my mama said weakly.

"What's wrong, Mama?" I questioned.

"It's nothing for you to worry about. I—"

"Don't start that shit, Mama. You wouldn't be here if it wasn't nothing wrong with you. I'm not a child; you don't have to lie just to fucking spare me," I said, full of irritation.

Under normal circumstances, I wouldn't dare ever talk to my mama like that, but these weren't normal circumstances. I hated when she tried to act like her health issues weren't a big deal just so she wouldn't upset me. When she first found out she was sick, she hid that shit for the longest until I accidentally found out about her condition.

"You better watch how you talk to my mama," Hendrix said from his seat on the opposite side of her hospital bed.

"Didn't I tell you not to say shit else to me? Fuck you keep trying me for, bitch? You don't believe fat meat greasy, huh? You want me to show you?" I asked him as I reached in the back of my pants for my gun I always kept on me.

I think my brother often forgot that I was halfway retarded and ain't give a fuck about shit. He always did the dumbest shit at the most unnecessary times. I was up here, trying to figure out what was going on with my mama, and he wanted to lose his life.

Before I could even remove my gun, my mama grabbed my arm and gave me a look that let me know she wasn't pleased. I loved my mama dearly, but she was going to have to stop coming to this nigga's rescue all the time.

Let this nigga get what the fuck he got coming to him.

"Boston, you know better," she chastised me.

"See, Mom, I told you. You always want to baby him and act as if he does no wrong. Boston has never had to suffer the consequences of his choices. That's the reason that he feels he can get away with doing whatever the hell he wants to," Hendrix whined like a little bitch.

"Make me suffer the consequences then, nigga. You so bad, why don't you do something about it?" I antagonized him as I walked over to where he was sitting.

"Boss, I'm trying to warn you, brother to brother, this ain't what you want. You know I know some very powerful people. I'll have your ass—"

That was all that Hendrix was able to get out before I tried to cave his fucking jaw in. I told his bitch ass about his fucking mouth and that threatening shit. He thought shit was sweet, so I was about to show him that it wasn't.

"Stop it, you two! I said stop, dammit!" my mom yelled at the top of her lungs.

That instantly caused the both of us to stop in motion and look at her with wide eyes. My mama was a very gentle person and had never raised her voice before. I knew she had to be pissed if she were yelling and cussing. My mama never let anything foul come out of her mouth.

"I'm about to fucking die, and you would think that, just for once, my two ignorant ass sons would be able to put this childish ass bullshit to the side and be there for me when I need them. I don't even know what to say to you two right now," she yelled.

By now, the nurses had rushed in here and were trying to get her to calm down. I stood there in shock at the fact that she said she was about to die.

The fuck did she mean?

"Mom—"

"Shut the hell up, Hendrix, and get out. Both of you, just leave," she cut him off.

With my head down, I solemnly walked out of her room, feeling like shit. For the first time in a long time, I fucked around and let my anger get the best of me. I took pride in saying that I'd been having my anger under control, but I was tired of Hendrix coming at me like I was some type of bitch or something. I strictly ignored his ass for a reason, but the bitch just wanted to get a rise out of me, and he got what he was asking for.

He'd better have been glad all I did was sock him in his fucking jaw because the old Boss, the Boss that I was before I had my daughter, would've just shot his ass. Sadly, I felt as if that ruthless nigga that I once was, was going to have to make a comeback. Call me crazy or whatever, but I felt a shift in the atmosphere, and this shit was about to get hectic.

§

"Look, Daddy! TT Dom!" Giselle yelled in excitement as she fought to hold the balloons that were about ten seconds from flying away.

Today was the day. My first baby—my oldest baby—was officially a college graduate. I was so proud that I could hardly contain the smile on my face. Freedom had done what she said she was going to do and made something out of herself. She did what I never did, and that was get a college degree.

"Gi-Gi!" Freedom yelled as she and Giselle ran into each other's arms. "Aww, I missed you, baby," she said as she smothered my baby with kisses.

"I missed you more. I got you some balloons. You like them?" Giselle asked as she damn near shoved the balloons in her auntie's face.

"I love them, sweetie, but I love you more," Freedom smiled.

"Ehem," I cleared my throat loudly. "So you don't see me standing here?" I asked.

"You are so dramatic. I was coming to you." Freedom playfully rolled her eyes as she walked over to me with Giselle still in her arms.

"Congrats, big head. I knew you could do it." I kissed her forehead.

"You sure do know how to make a girl smile." She laughed as she took the flowers and envelope from me.

Freedom looked around, and I noticed the smile slowly fade from her face. I hadn't got around to telling her that Mama was in the hospital, because I didn't want to ruin her special day for her. I knew that was exactly who she was looking for.

"What's wrong?" I asked, playing it off.

"Where's Mama?" she asked.

"Mama couldn't make it, Dom. She's—"

"What's wrong with her? Don't bullshit me either, Boston," she cut me off.

Since Freedom was the only girl and the youngest, she and our Mama were very close. It was crazy because she was a daddy's girl and a mommy's girl at the same time. Everyone had her little ass spoiled.

"Her Hepatitis C turned into Cirrhosis. You know Mama, so you know she hid that shit from us, and now, she has liver failure."

Ever since I was little, and ever since Freedom had been on this earth, my mom had been very sick. Freedom was actually what she called her miracle baby due to doctors suggesting that she couldn't have any more babies after me. She'd had three miscarriages before she was able to carry Freedom to full term. That was another reason her ass was so spoiled; she'd made it through just when my mama was about to give up all hope and stop trying to have a baby.

My mama had been diagnosed with diabetes at a young age, but they didn't have the resources that we had these days, so it went untreated for a while. That caused some damage to her liver, which resulted in her developing Hepatitis C. She had been dealing with that for a while, but we thought everything was under control until she hid from us that she had liver failure with not that much longer to live.

I was going to leave that last part out, though, because I knew Freedom wouldn't be able to handle that. I had already sprung too much on her, but she insisted on knowing.

"Why nobody told me this shit? Y'all got me living all the way down here in Louisiana and got me in the dark about everything that's going on back home. That shit ain't fair, Boston. Where the hell is Hendrix? What's his reasoning for not being here?" Freedom ranted.

"Fuck his bitch ass," I spat.

Freedom sucked her teeth before closing her hand in front of her face as if she were telling herself to calm down. Being the dramatic lil' brat that she was, she threw her hair over her shoulders before grabbing Giselle's hand.

"You know what? I don't have time for this. Let's just go so you can spend some money on me and my princess. Then, we can hurry up and get home so I can get to my mommy. You and yo' ugly ass brother probably up there driving her crazy with y'all bullshit. Come on!" Freedom yelled as she and Giselle walked off.

I had to say a quick prayer for Freedom's wellbeing so I wouldn't have to fuck her up. The sooner I got her back to Detroit and out of my way, the better.

Choyce

"*F*uck you over there doing?" Boss asked with a scowl on his face.

He had been gone to Louisiana for two days now for his sister's graduation, but he'd called me on FaceTime every day to talk to Zamani and me. Even though I hated to admit it, Boss was starting to become a very important part of my life. The crazy thing about it was the shit didn't even happen on purpose. What started off as innocent, as us just planning little play dates for the girls, unexpectedly blossomed into more between us, and we both felt it no matter how much we tried to fight it.

"Packing my bag for work," I told him.

"Work, huh? That's what you call that?" he asked with that fucked up look still on his face.

"Don't start that. Anyway. What you doing? When you coming home?" I switched subjects.

On more than one occasion, Boss had no problems expressing to me how he felt about me leaving the club. Whenever I mentioned it, or he brought up the way I made my money, he always had something slick to say. Even though I already had plans on eventually leaving the strip club, I didn't have the means to do so right now.

I still had to finish getting my GED then save up enough money to pay for my classes when I enrolled in college. So, in reality, I couldn't just quit stripping on a limb like that all because he wanted me to.

"Why? You miss me?" Boss asked a question of his own with a little smirk on his face.

"Maybe. Not really," I shrugged.

"You lying; you know you miss a nigga. Aye, let me see them titties real quick."

I just shook my head at him even though I knew he was serious. Boss was freaky as hell, to say the least. He was always feeling up on me, smacking my ass, or rubbing his dick on me. The only time he could contain himself was when the girls were around, and he could barely do it then.

"Boss, I'm not—"

"Just let me see 'em, man. Why you always acting so shy? I'm gon' have to fix that shit," he said.

Sighing, I did as he asked and exposed myself to him. He had a smile on his face that resembled the one a child wore on Christmas morning as they opened their presents. After figuring he'd had a good enough look, I pulled my shirt and bra back down.

"Ooohweee! As soon as I touch down, I'm coming to suck on them titties," he said with a straight face.

"You so nasty," I laughed.

"I'm so serious," he informed me.

I was about to say something, but the sound of my doorbell

ringing caught me off guard. I knew it couldn't have been Jamaica, because she was at her house with Zamani. Plus, she had a key, so she would just walk right in. I didn't get visitors, so I was puzzled on who could've been at my door.

"Who the fuck is that?" Boss asked.

"I don't know; hold on," I told him as I rushed out of my room to go see who was at the door.

Looking through the peephole, I stood there confused for a few, trying to figure just exactly what the hell was going on.

"I'll call you back." I hung up before Boss could say anything.

I swung the door open with force and looked around to see if I could spot the camera crew or something because I just knew I had to be on an episode of Punk'd, or somebody was playing a trick on me. This shit was not realistic.

"Uhh, what you doing here?" I questioned skeptically.

"I just came to check on you," Turelle said.

I looked at him through squinted eyes because I was having a hard time believing that he gave a fuck about checking on me. His ass didn't even think to stop by to check on his daughter, but now, all of a sudden, he was here to check on me.

Fuck outta here.

"Stop playing with me, Turelle. What the hell do you want? Why are you really here?" I asked once again.

"Can I come in or…"

I must've had 'Boo Boo the damn fool' written across my

forehead if Turelle thought he was coming in my house. This nigga barely allowed me to step foot on his damn porch, but he wanted me to let him into my humble abode. In the words of a very wise man, hell naw to the naw, naw, naw.

"Bye, Turelle," I said as I tried to shut the door.

Stopping it with his foot, he forced it back open.

"Look, Choyce, I just wanted to give you a little warning about the company you seem to have been keeping. Don't play dumb, because I already peeped the shit. That nigga Boss ain't no fucking good. He come with a lot of bullshit that I know for a fact you not gon' be ready for. Just ask the last bitch he got close to. Everything he comes in contact with, he destroys it, so if I were you, I would cut that shit short, and you damn sure better not have that nigga around my daughter," Turelle had the audacity to say.

I let out a little laugh because this shit was comical as fuck. "That daughter that you claim is not yours, that you don't do shit for, and that you want nothing to do with?" I continued to laugh. "Turelle, you got this all fucked up. I'm grown and single as hell, so whoever I choose to spend my time with is none of your business. Boss has done way more for Zamani in the little time he's known her than you've done since she's been on this earth. Don't bring yo' stupid ass around me with that bullshit no more." I slammed the door in his face.

Making sure the door was locked, I huffed as I made my way back up the stairs so I could finish packing my bag and take a little nap before it was time for me to go to the club. Minutes after the fact, I was still in shock that Turelle had had the audacity to come at me with that bullshit.

For the past four years, that nigga hadn't been worried 'bout me, Zamani, or what I had going on, but now, all of a sudden, he had something to say. I needed for him to find the highest cliff he could and jump off that bitch, head first.

§

Bang, bang, bang!

I hadn't even been lying down for a full thirty minutes before I somebody banging on my door like the damn police. I jumped up out my sleep and glanced at the clock noting that it was almost eleven o'clock at night.

Bang, bang, bang!

"What the fuck!" I yelled as I jumped out of the bed.

I went straight to my closet and grabbed the metal bat I kept in there before marching down the stairs. When I made it to the door, I checked the peephole, but it was covered.

This nigga is bold.

Snatching the door open, I put the bat in the air, ready to swing, until I saw who was standing on the other side.

"Boss!" I squealed before jumping in his arms.

"The fuck was you about to do with that?" he asked through a laugh as he kicked the bat I had dropped out of the way as he walked into the house with me still in his arms.

Boss held me with one arm while shutting the door with the other. He carried me as if I weighed nothing, which to him, I probably didn't.

"I was about to fuck you up," I told him honestly. "What you doing here? I just talked to you, and you ain't say nothing about coming home," I said, looking at him like he was crazy.

"I came home early this morning. I just had to get my sister settled in and check on some business before I came to see you," he said as he sat on the couch with me on his lap.

Every time I looked into Boss' honey-colored eyes, I got lost in them. His eyes held a story that I had yet to figure out. He wasn't into going into detail about his life or opening up. The only thing I knew about him was the fact that Giselle's mother was on drugs, and he was raising her on his own.

He had this big ass wall built up that I was having the toughest time trying to crack. Every time I thought I was getting him to open up, he would shun away and direct it back towards me.

"Where's Giselle?" I asked as a ran my finger over the tattoos that peeked out the top of his shirt.

"I left her with her worrisome ass auntie. I was going to end up choking one of them, so I had to get the fuck on," he said while rubbing my booty.

"You're crazy."

I tried to get up, but he grabbed me by my waist to hold me in place. I looked at him sideways with a questioning look, but he just looked at me intently.

"Boss, I gotta go," I told him.

Ignoring me, he ran his hands up my tank top, softly tickling my skin. He grabbed the bottom of my shirt before quickly pulling it over my head before I could stop him. Using one hand, he reached behind me and unsnapped my bra with the precision of a pro.

Like a hungry nursing infant, Boss latched onto my right nipple while twisting the left one between his fingers. I tried to stifle a moan, but the sensation I was feeling was unbearable. Unconsciously, I started slowly grinding my hips into him, which caused Boss to instantly stop what he was doing.

"Wh-what's wrong?" I asked.

"I know you feel that big muthafucka growing under you. If I was you, I wouldn't grind that fat ass pussy on me unless you want this fucking anaconda in yo' snake hole," he said through a breath.

I had to bite my lip to keep from smiling. His mouth was so foul, and he ain't care what the hell flew out of it, but I think that was one of the main things I liked about him. His no-fucks-given attitude was sexy as fuck.

"Is that right?" I asked as I started grinding once again.

Suddenly, a look came over his face as he got up from the couch with me still in his arms. I let out a yelp as he slapped my ass as he jogged up the stairs and to the bedroom. He walked me over to the bed and laid me down gently before kissing my neck as he dug in his pocket.

He came out with a gold wrapper, and I already knew what time it was. I wasn't going to ask him what the hell he was doing walking around with a condom in his pocket, because after all, he wasn't my man, but my look must've said it all because he gave me a smile.

Standing up straight, he dropped his pants along with his boxers, and his dick bounced out like it had hydraulics or something.

I had felt it plenty times before when it was on soft, but this was a totally different ballgame. His cocky ass knew he was walking around with a monster in his pants because he gave me an ugly little smirk as he rolled the condom on. After he had it on and secured, he kissed his way up my body as he hovered over me, placing the head of his dick at my opening.

"You ready?" he asked just above a whisper.

Fuck no!

Nodding my head, I prepared myself for what was to come, but he never moved an inch.

"I don't speak sign language, Choyce. You gotta open ya mouth when you speaking to me. If you want this muthafucka, you gotta let me know," he told me.

Honestly, I wasn't sure if I was ready. Of course, I wasn't a virgin, but I hadn't had sex since before my daughter was born, and I had only been with one man. I had sworn off all men and put all my focus into my daughter and making money. Boss was the first man I had even entertained since Turelle broke my heart.

I didn't know what this meant for Boss and I after we crossed this line. Were we going to be together? Friends with benefits? Or just fuck buddies? Maybe these were questions I should've been asking beforehand, but it was too late to turn back now.

"I want it. … I'm ready," I let him know.

Boss eased his way in, but he was met with some resistance while I was hit with pain. He did a slow grind until he was all the way in, and I let go of the breath I forgot I was holding.

"You good?" he asked.

"Yeah."

As if that were all he needed to hear, Boss took my legs and put them on his shoulder as he hit me with some deadly slow strokes. Out of nowhere, he picked up the speed and started fucking the shit outta me.

"Oh, shit, Boss!" I moaned.

I'd heard stories about bitches saying they could feel the dick in their stomachs, but now, I was a living witness. This nigga was hitting spots that should've been illegal. Slowly but surely, I could feel him fucking the common sense out of me. He definitely had the type of dick that would make a bitch dumb and act crazy.

Maybe I should've left his ass where I found him.

"Shit," Boss groaned. "Turn over," he instructed.

Doing as he said, I turned over and tooted my ass up in the air, but he pushed my back down so I was laying on my stomach. Kissing each of my ass cheeks, he slowly slid back in and paused before he went right back to fucking the shit out of me.

"Fuuuuuck, Boss!" I yelled out as I reached back so he could take some out.

That was obviously the wrong move on my behalf because he took my arms around and folded them behind me as he continued rearranging my guts.

"This my pussy now. If you ever give it up, I'll kill you and that nigga," Boss grunted.

I guess he was expecting a response because he grabbed a handful of my hair and yanked my hair back but not too hard to hurt me.

"You fucking hear me, Choyce? On my dead daddy, I'll kill you," he reiterated.

"Yes! Yes!" I yelled as I was hit with a body-rocking orgasm.

The next thing I knew, Boss was grunting, and I felt a wet, sticky substance on my ass. I turned around to see this nigga nutting on my ass. Long gone was the condom. I was too tired to say anything, so I just weakly lay there as he got out of the bed and made his way to the bathroom.

I had already started dozing off when I felt the warm rag on my ass and him opening my legs to wipe my honey pot for me. I jumped a little due to it being so sensitive.

"My bad," Boss chuckled.

Moments later, he returned and plopped down on the bed next to me, pulling me into his arms. I lay my head on his chest and went to sleep, forgetting that I was supposed to be at the club.

Johann

"*Y*o, B! Where you—"

"Ahhh!"

My question was cut off by a loud ass scream followed by a towel dropping and a naked body on display.

"My bad," I said as I immediately turned on my heels and walked out of the kitchen.

"Han?"

Stopping in my tracks, I slowly turned around to the sound of the familiar voice. Freedom now had the towel wrapped around her body again as she stood there in shock. She looked as if she didn't know how to feel about seeing me, and I felt the same way about seeing her. It had been years since the last time I'd laid eyes on her. I knew Boss said he was going to her graduation, but he said nothing about her coming here.

"Hanny, wait!" she yelled as she ran after me and grabbed my arm once I took off again.

"Fuck off me!" I shoved her harder than I intended to, and she fell to the ground.

With a look of sadness, Freedom picked herself off the floor and looked at me in disbelief. Never in my years of knowing her had I ever put my hands on her not even to jack her little ass up. Even though I kinda felt bad right now, all the other emotions I was feeling trumped that.

"You promised you'd never hit me, Johann."

"Just like you promised you would always be there for me. I guess we just some lying ass muthafuckas, huh?" I spat.

"I had no choice, Johann! Boss sent me away to go to school. Besides, do you think it was easy for me to watch the dude I loved mourning over another bitch?" Freedom spat.

"Watch yo' fucking mouth," I warned her as I grabbed her by her jaws as tight as I could.

I know, I know, you probably sitting there, scratching ya head, tryna figure out what the fuck is going on. This shit ain't really easy to explain, but I'll try.

The situation with Freedom and I was never supposed to happen. I had too much love and loyalty for Boss to ever come at his little sister like that, but shit happened, and you couldn't help who you fell for. What started off as some innocent ass shit like me venting to her when I felt I had no one else to talk to or didn't want to be judged eventually led to us catching feelings for one another.

I knew Freedom was off limits; not only was she my best friend's sister, but she was also young as hell. When we started fucking around, I was twenty years old, and she was only sixteen. To make matters worse, I was already in a relationship. I had too much love and respect for Freedom to ever have her as my side bitch, but every time I tried to cut her off, something kept pulling me back.

Even when I was sent off to the army, I tried to cut her off, but Freedom wasn't having it. She hit me with some shit about her being pregnant, but I accused her of lying. Before I was deployed, we had gotten into a big fight, and she said she was going to finally tell Boss that we had been sneaking around behind his back. I told her if she did that, I was going to kick her ass, and her best bet would be to get an abortion because she was going to be a single mother anyway.

I ain't mean none of the shit I was saying, but Freedom always knew how to push my damn buttons. Just like she was the only person who really knew me, she knew exactly what to do and what to say to set me off. Forgetting that Freedom was still a child; she did the most childish thing she could have done, and that was tell my girl she was pregnant by me.

Not even a month after I came home, I found out from my girl that Freedom went ahead with the abortion. Me and my girl got into a big ass fight where she took my daughter and left the house. In a fit of rage, she ran a red light, which caused her to get into a car accident where her car flipped. She and my daughter lost their lives upon impact.

That was the worst day of my life. I was already going through shit from the war. Then, to come home and experience that trauma was too much for me to handle. Freedom and I had barely had any communication since the funeral, then all of a sudden, she just up and left for the south.

"Get the fuck off me."

Whap!

Freedom slapped the shit out of my ass before taking off for the stairs. I stood there for a minute, waiting for the stinging sensation on the side of my face to subside before I went after her ass. Running up the stairs, two at a time, I quickly made my way to one of the guest rooms Boss had set up in his house. She wasn't in that one, so I made my way to the next one. After about the third door, I tried to turn the knob, but it was locked.

"Open the fucking door!" I yelled.

Silence.

"Freedom, I'm giving you to the count of three to open this fucking door, or I'ma kick this bitch in. You know I don't give a fuck about dealing with yo' brother. One, … two, … three."

Bow!

Freedom thought I was a fucking joke. She had been gone so long that she forgot I really didn't have it all. When I said I would kick this bitch in, I meant just that. Boss was just going to have to kick my ass for old and new. The cat was going to be let out of the bag today. Either way, I was going to make my way into this room.

Bow!

I kicked it again with all my might since she refused to open the door. Just as I was about to lift my leg up again, the door swung open, and Freedom hit my black ass with a plastic hanger.

"Ahh! The fuck wrong with yo' crazy ass?" I yelled as I shoved her crazy ass back and grabbed the hanger from her.

"I hate you! I fucking hate you!" she yelled as she jumped on me.

This crazy ass girl was hitting me all in the back of my head, my neck, and my back. I had no choice but to body slam her ass when she bit my neck. She bounced off the bed like a fucking rag doll, but even then, that ain't calm her ass down. That just seemed to fuel her already raging fire. I had to laugh because this shit wasn't doing shit but bringing back memories.

Freedom and I used to fight like dogs then fuck like them as well right after. It was just something about her little aggressive ass thinking she could whoop my ass that made my dick hard, like right now for instance.

Grabbing at the lace panties she had put on, I ripped them bitches off with no warning. Freedom's eyes bucked, and she tried to fight me harder, but I knew that shit was just a show. She knew like I knew that I had just what it took to calm her little feisty ass down.

"Stop, Johann! I'm not playing with you!" she yelled while trying to tighten her legs together as I grabbed her hands in one of my hands and used the other to part her legs while kissing down her body.

"Well, I'm about to play with you." I smirked as I rubbed her clit.

"Don't touch me; I hate you!"

"But you love this tongue, though." I smirked as I pushed her legs back and latched onto her clit with my mouth.

"Uhh, baby." Freedom moaned as she placed her hand on my head.

"Stop fucking touching me!" I snapped as I slapped her hand away.

"I-but-shit! I love you, Hanny!"

I laughed to myself because just a few seconds ago, she was hollering about how she hated me. Now, I had that ass singing a different tune. I was no bragger or anything of the sort, but my head game was the shit. I was literally only two minutes in, and I had her ass shaking like she was having convulsions.

That wasn't good enough for me, though. Freedom was grabbing at the sheets and slapping the fuck out of the bed. She tried to push my head away, but once again, I slapped her hand away.

"Baby, pleaseeee?" she begged.

Still not satisfied, I took two of my fingers and stuck them in her tight pussy as I licked and sucked on her clit harder. I used my fingers to fuck the shit out of her until I had her ass squirting.

"Yesssss!"

"There it is." I smiled as I got up, wiping my mouth with my shirt.

Freedom just laid there, sprawled out across the bed, looking crazy, as she fought to catch her breath. She had a big ass wet spot under her, and I patted myself on the back at my handiwork.

Grabbing her by the throat, I pressed firmly. "Put yo' muthafucking hands on me again, and see if I don't fuck you up," I threatened her with all sincerity in my heart before walking out.

"Wait. … Where you going?" she asked, out of breath.

"Where the fuck you think? I'm not about to start this shit back up with you again, Freedom. Don't get me wrong, I do miss that sweet little pussy, but it's not worth all the trouble it comes with," I let her know.

No matter how much I loved Freedom, fucking with her caused me to lose too much, and I still hadn't gotten over that shit. I was still pissed at her ass for killing my damn baby. I would always love Freedom—there was no denying that shit—but the two of us just weren't meant to be together. I was too grown to be sneaking around with a female because of how her brother might've felt about us.

Boss

"Taste this," Choyce said as she put a spoonful of sauce up to my mouth.

Tasting the sauce, I nodded my head approvingly as I watched a big smile spread across her face. Tonight, she had invited Giselle and me over to cook for us. She had even extended the invitation to Freedom, but I quickly had to shut that down. Don't get me wrong, I liked Choyce, but I didn't have an idea of exactly what we had going on.

She was cool as hell, I liked her vibe, she had a good head on her shoulders, and the sex was out of this world, but I wasn't ready for a girlfriend or anything like one. For right now, the two of us were just chillin'—nothing more.

"Aye, bring me a beer when you come back out the kitchen," I told her.

"Okay," she said before walking away.

I sat back on the couch and put my feet up on the coffee table as I flipped through the movies on the Fire Stick for me something to watch. This was the first time in a long time that I'd had some time to just relax and not have to worry about the stress of my street affairs.

Just then, my phone started ringing.

Spoke too soon.

"Yea?" I answered.

"Boston, we've been doing business for years, right?" Juarez, one of my customers, said.

"Yeah, and?"

"So you know I must trust you a lot if I've been in business with you this long."

"Just get to the point, Juarez. I don't have time for all this extra shit," I said, getting irritated.

"I'm just trying to figure out why, after all these years, you would try to cheat me. My supply was low, and I don't appreciate it," he informed me.

I pulled the phone away from my ear and looked at it like this nigga was stupid. I didn't know if he'd been doing the shit he was buying or what, but I knew he had to be high if he were coming at me with this bullshit.

"Aye, I'm not in the mood for these games and shit. You—"

"Boston, like I said, I trust you. A lot. So, I trust that you will figure this issue out before it causes some very unnecessary problems between us. I would not lie nor play with you about such matters. It's the respect that I have for you that allowed me to call and speak with you about the situation instead of acting on it first," Juarez let me know.

The situation wasn't funny, but I had to laugh at the fact that Juarez called himself trying to threaten me. He was a little spoiled ass daddy's boy who had never put in work a day in his life. Everything he had, he'd inherited from his father, who I was doing business with before his untimely death. I would've taken the threat more seriously if it had come from his father because Juarez was as soft as mashed potatoes and didn't want it with me.

"I'll look into it, and Juarez, don't ever in yo' fucking life threaten me like I'm some pussy ass nigga. Find yo'self in a situation yo' daddy's reputation won't be able to get you out of," I let him know just as Choyce walked in the room with my beer.

I hung up on his bitch ass and threw my phone on the couch next to me as she stood there with a questioning look.

"What was that about?" she asked.

"Nothing you need to worry yo' sexy ass about," I told her as I slapped her on her juicy ass.

"Hmm, okay," she shrugged. "The food is done. I'm about to get the girls so they can wash their hands," she said.

"Cool."

While Choyce went to get the girls cleaned up, I made my way to the kitchen to see what her ass had whipped up. The whole time she was in there cooking, she wouldn't allow me to step foot in the kitchen. I thought the shit was funny because my mom was the same way when she was cooking.

I reached for one of the pots to peek under it when I heard little footsteps coming into the kitchen.

"Did you wash your hands while you in here, sneaking in my pots?" Choyce fussed.

"I was just about to do that," I told her through a smile.

"Mhmm." She cut her eyes at me as she got some plates out of the cabinet.

I felt something tugging at my pant leg and looked down to see Zamani's little cute self standing there, looking up at me with those big eyes she got from her mama.

"What's up, lil' mama?" I asked as I picked her up.

"I draw you picture," she said sweetly as she held up a piece of paper.

I took the picture from her and smiled at the little squiggly lines in different colors that consisted of the picture she drew for me. At the bottom of it, I saw she'd tried to spell her name. It wasn't a lot that got to me, but I couldn't lie; this shit touched a nigga's heart.

"Thank you, lil' mama, it's beautiful. Just like you," I said as I kissed her forehead.

Out the corner of my eye, I could see Choyce smiling from ear to ear. She and Giselle were on the other side of the kitchen in their own little world as Giselle helped her fixed the plates. This was how it always seemed to be whenever the four of us got together. Zamani would be right by my side, and Giselle would be stuck to Choyce like glue.

I would've been lying if I said I wasn't slightly jealous, but at the same time, the shit was cute. Anybody that could work their way into my mean ass daughter's heart was already five steps ahead of the game.

§

"Who this?" I asked through a groan.

I glanced over at Choyce as she stirred in her sleep, but she didn't wake up.

"Boss, it's me. … It's G."

I pulled my phone away from my ear to check the time, and it was damn near four thirty in the morning. I hadn't heard from Gianna since that day I had to get on her ass about her popping up at my mama's house.

"Fuck you calling me this late for? You high?" I asked.

"What? No, no, I told you I was clean, but I kinda need you, Boss. I'm scared, and I don't have no one else to call. I promise I'm not on no bullshit, just please," she begged.

I pinched the bridge of my nose as I thought about the situation. A big ass part of me wanted to hang up the phone on her ass, roll over, and go back to sleep, but a small, tiny part of me was telling me to hear her out.

"Never mind, I'll just—"

"Text me the location; I'm on my way. If this some bullshit, I promise, I'm pumping lead into yo' dumb ass." I hung up before she could respond.

I lightly moved Choyce's arm from around me and crept out of the bed so I wouldn't wake her. I threw on a pair of basketball shorts and a hoodie I had at her house before sliding my feet into some Nike slides. I stuffed my phone into the pocket of my hoodie before making my way out of the room.

Walking down the hallway, I stopped by Zamani's room and

checked on the girls before leaving. They were sound asleep, so I slowly closed the door and made my way out of the house. Pulling my phone out of my pocket, I dialed up my right-hand man.

"Nigga finally made time to crawl out the pussy, huh?" he answered.

"Shut yo' ass up," I slightly laughed.

"What's wrong? I know yo' ass ain't calling me this late … or early just because you miss me," Han said.

I knew, more than likely, Han would be up at these hours. Ever since he came back from the war, he rarely slept past three o'clock in the morning due to his crazy ass dreams.

"I need you to take a ride with me, playboy," I let him know.

"Pull up; I'm ready," he said.

"Aight."

That was exactly why Han was my right-hand man. He stayed ready at all times, and he never asked questions whenever I needed him. Twenty minutes later, I was pulling up to Han's house, and this crazy ass nigga was standing outside, looking like the grim reaper, dressed in all black from head to toe.

He briskly walked over to the car and slid in, adjusting the seat so he was damn near laying down before lighting up the blunt he had placed behind his ear.

"Sis let yo' ass out the house this late?" Han asked before taking a puff.

I cut my eyes at him before answering. "I'm a grown ass man,

Johann. Not to mention, I'm single. Don't get this shit twisted," I reminded him.

"It seems that the only one who got the shit twisted is you, nigga. Y'all spending damn near every day together, going on family dates, spending nights at each other's houses, Gi-Gi loves her, and her daughter loves you. Shit, it sounds like y'all damn near in a relationship to me." Han shrugged as he passed me the blunt.

I just rubbed the back of my head as I thought about the shit Han just said. Was it wrong for me to want to be in the company of a woman and feel that companionship without wanting to be in a committed relationship? I had tried that route before, and the shit slapped me dead in the face.

Choyce and I were just chilling. I wouldn't lie and say that I didn't feel something for her; it wasn't love or none of that shit, but I had some type of feelings for the kid. Not to mention, her daughter had worked her way into my heart as well. I just wasn't trying to be tied down right now.

"Everything ain't what it seems, pimp," I let him know as I took the blunt.

"Nah, you can't make her suffer for the last bitch's fuck ups, because if the shoe was on the other foot, you wouldn't have it. Keep playing, and you gon' fuck around and let another nigga snatch her ass up because you're scared. Shit, that nigga just might be me."

"Yeah, aight, get yo' ass beat," I told him.

"Damn, we fighting over pussy now? Shit that good?" Han asked with wide eyes.

"Fucking sensational, nigga. I would go into detail, but I respect her ass too much. Just know she got the type of shit that will make you kill a nigga over it," I said as flashbacks of the sexcapade I'd just had with Choyce earlier flashed in my mind.

"Respect." Han smiled while giving me dap just as we pulled up to the address Gianna sent me. "Nigga, the fuck type shit you got going on? A nigga owe you some money or something?"

Pulling out my phone, I hit the number that Gianna had previously called me from to call and let her know that I was here, but it was going straight to voicemail. I instantly started feeling like this was some setup shit. A part of me thought she would never do no shit like that to me, but I never thought she would cheat on me either, but she did, so I wasn't putting shit past her ass at this point.

"Come on," I told Han as I reached in my secret compartment of my car for my gun I kept hidden in there.

Following my lead, Han got out of the car with his twin desert eagles at his side. The sun wasn't up yet, so it was still dark as we slowly crept up to the house on Joy Road with our weapons on display, ready for whatever. The front door swung open, and Han had his gun aimed, ready to fire before I stopped him.

"Chill, Han!" I slapped his gun down just as Gianna ran into my arms.

"You came?" she said as if she couldn't believe it.

I didn't bother to respond as I led the way back to my awaiting truck while still checking my surroundings. My eyes landed on Han, and he had a questioning look on his face, but he never opened his mouth to speak on the situation. He just shoved his guns back in his waistline while following behind us to the car.

It was dead silent when we all got back in the truck. Gianna knew I had a strict rule about speaking any type of business in the car. That shit just wasn't safe. I had heard about too many situations where niggas got caught up because they were too busy running their mouths in a car where they thought they were safe but had no idea their shit was bugged the whole time.

I drove her ass straight to the nearest hotel. Taking her to my crib wasn't even an option, especially with Freedom being there. My sister already wanted to beat her ass, and I had no doubts she would finally get the job done if I had her and Gianna in the same room at the same time.

I peeled off a few bills and sent her ass in there to get a room.

"Come back out to get me when you get the key," I instructed.

The whole time, Han just sat there, stone faced, looking straight ahead until Gianna disappeared into the building. He finally turned to look at me, and his face read nothing but disappointment.

"Speak yo' peace," I told him.

"You really about to get caught up with this bitch again, B?" he spat, full of hate. "I know that's Giselle's mama and all that, but the fuck is this shit here?"

The way Han was speaking with so much emotion, you would've thought *he* was the one that Gianna did wrong. I couldn't front; he was asking some very valid questions that I was sitting here trying to figure out the answers to myself.

"Han, shit ain't even like that. She called me—"

"And you came running? You ain't ask no questions? This bitch fucked another nigga, in yo' shit, got pregnant by another nigga, and hid the fact that she butchered the shit because she ain't know if it was yours or the other nigga's. Not to mention, it wasn't some random ass nigga; it was your whole ass brother. Now, if that don't scream 'leave that trifling ass bitch alone,' then I don't know what to tell you. You my man, a hunnit grand, but whatever the fuck is going on, I'm involving myself because of you. I don't give a fuck about what happens to her," Han let me know just as Gianna stepped out the door of the hotel.

The elevator ride up to her room was a very quiet one. Nobody spoke a word to each other. It was evident that Gianna had been holding true to her word and had been managing to stay clean this time around. She had gained her weight back in all the right places, so she was starting to look like the old Gianna.

When we reached her room, I wasted no time getting down to business. The sun was about to be coming up in a few, and I wanted to make it to the house before any of my girls could wake up.

"Aight, tell me what the fuck you had me climbing out of my bed at three o'clock in the morning for?" I questioned.

"Your brother sent some dudes after me," Gianna said.

I stood there emotionless as I tried to figure out exactly what this had to do with me and why I was here again.

"And? What the fuck that gotta do with me?" I asked, already losing my patience.

"He sent them after me because I didn't have any info on you,

Boss! Hendrix has been trying for years to get me to give up some dirt on you, but I wouldn't tell him shit. How do you think I got addicted to this shit? You think I just woke up one day and said today is a good day to try drugs? Hell no! Hendrix tried to force me to be with him and give up some info on you to get you locked up, but when I refused to do it, he beat my ass and stuck a fucking needle in my arm. Think about the shit, Boss. You never allowed any of your people to sell to me, so how do you think I got my fix? Hendrix has always been lurking in the shadows. Whenever I tried to get clean, he sent some dudes after me to fuck me up and pump the drugs back in me," Gianna explained.

I had always been a good judge of character and could always tell when somebody was lying to me, especially Gianna. She always did this little thing with her mouth when she was lying, and I watched her closely, and not once did she do it.

"Why the fuck you ain't tell me this shit, G?"

"How, Boss? Whenever I tried to tell you some shit, you wasn't tryna hear me. I tried to tell you about your brother, but you always blew me off," she said.

I glanced over at Han, but he had a blank expression on his face as if he could care less about what Gianna was saying. He sat quietly on the opposite side of the room with his hands stuffed in his pockets, slouched down in his seat.

"When was the last time Hendrix came around?" I asked.

"He came by the house today. He comes by at least three times a week, asking about you. He had his goon squad with him today, and that's why I called you. I'm just tired of the bullshit that he comes with.

That nigga is crazy, Boss," she said.

Nodding my head, I made my way towards the door with Han in tow.

"Chill out here for a few days. Lay low. I'll check into the situation and come by to check on you," I threw over my shoulder.

"Umm, Boss."

"What, G?" I asked through a sigh.

"You think I could see Giselle?" she asked.

Han let out a low whistle, and I let out a little laugh. "That's some shit I'll have to think hard about."

Even though I could see that Gianna was fighting hard to stay clean this time, I had to make sure she wasn't caught up in any shit that would put my daughter at risk. Above anything else, I was going to have to have a conversation with Giselle to see how she felt about seeing her mom. If that were something she wanted to do, then we could go from there. Either way, I was going to support her decision one hunnit percent.

Turk

I took a swig from my bottle of Henny as I used the back of my hand to wipe the sweat from my brow. It was the end of May, which meant that it was time for the annual cookout Boss sponsored every year for Memorial Day. This was really the only time of the year where you could catch Boss's ugly ass in the hood for more than a few minutes.

He was supposed to be this big nigga around the hood and doing this and that but never came back to show his hood any love. The nigga was just soft as fuck if you asked me. How the hell you scared of the same hood who made you the nigga that you were?

This bad ass redbone across from where I was standing caught my attention. She was so engrossed in whatever was going on in her phone that she had no idea of what was going on around her. Licking my lips, I took another swig of the liquor as I made my way over to her.

"How you doing, beautiful?" I asked.

She ran her eyes over me before tossing her hair over her shoulder and looking back down at her phone.

"Hi," she said dryly without even looking at me.

One of them stuck up bitches.

"You not too friendly, huh?" I asked, trying to get a conversation out of her.

"Nope," she replied, still not looking up.

I had to let out a little laugh because this shit was funny. Never had I had bitch play me like this. Getting bitches had never been a problem for me. It was just something about the kid that drew the bitches in and had them under my spell.

She looked up from her phone slowly with the stank face as she pushed her sunglasses down her nose. Her doing that caused her to look real familiar, but I couldn't place her.

"Can I help you with something? You need something? Or ... what?" she asked.

"Nah, I'm just tryna get a little conversation up out cha. I ain't never seen you around here before. What's yo' name?" I inquired as I stepped closer to her.

Just as she opened her mouth to reply, an annoying ass voice accompanied by somebody shoulder bumping me interrupted her.

"Aye, shut this shit down," Han said.

Of course, his hating ass wouldn't be too far behind. He was always lurking in the shadows somewhere, on some hating ass shit. The nigga just didn't want to admit it, but he knew like everybody else knew that he was jealous of me. I brought in more revenue than he ever could, and he hated that shit. The only reason he got the position that he did was because of the history he and Boss had. Like I said before, that nigga ain't never really put in no work; neither of 'em had.

"I'm talking," lil' mama said with an attitude.

"Do it really look like I give a fuck? Stop fucking playing with me, and do what the fuck I said," Han damn near growled at her ass.

"Why you feeling so beefy, Johann? I told you I'm talking, and you being real disrespectful to my friend right now. Gon' somewhere with all that extra shit."

"Han, look, you need to chill, nigga. Shit ain't even all that deep for you to be—"

"Fuck is you even speaking to me for right now, bitch?" Han spun around, looking like the devil himself. "I'm talking to her. The safest thing fo' yo' ugly ass to do right now is to walk away while I'm giving you the chance to," he said as he reached for the gun in his waistband.

"What? No, okay, Johann, you doing too much right now. Let's go," Redbone said as she grabbed his arm and pulled him away.

Using his hand like a pistol, Han acted as if he were pulling the trigger as to indicate he was going to kill my ass. I always said that nigga was crazy, but he had life fucked up if he thought I was going to keep letting him come at me like he was crazy. Today was the last straw; I wasn't taking his shit no more. If it were gunplay that Han wanted, then that was what his bitch ass was gon' get.

Shaking my head, I walked over to the cooler to get myself a beer since my Henny was now gone. Boss was posted up nearby on the phone. I was paying his ass no attention to his ass until I heard some shit that piqued my interest.

"We gon' have some major ass problems if you don't bring yo' ass down here, Choyce. Where my baby at? I know she miss me. Yo' hating ass just don't want us to be great. Put Mani on the phone," he said into the phone.

The fuck?

I knew Choyce and Boss had something going on, but I ain't think shit was that deep between them. I had specifically instructed that bitch to keep this nigga away from my daughter, but she must've thought I was a joke or something. She was about to find out just how serious I was. I was so lost in my thoughts that I ain't even notice Boss had gotten off the phone.

"Aye, Boss, you still fucking with Choyce?" I asked.

"Fuck you in my business for?" his cocky ass asked.

"I'm just warning you. I wouldn't trust that bitch as far as I can throw her," I let him know.

Boss smacked his lips and waved me off. "Gon' with that shit, Turk. You don't even know her."

It was obvious that Choyce didn't hip Boss to the little fact that we knew each other, let alone had a child together. I couldn't let my nigga go out like that, so I had to let him know just what type of bitch he was fucking with.

"I know her way better than you think I do, Boss," I told him.

I could tell by the look in his eyes that I had him hooked with that line. All I had to do now was reel him in and go for the kill.

"Fuck is that supposed to mean?" he asked, getting all hostile.

Got em.

"It means that Choyce and I are very acquainted. I was the one who broke her little chocolate ass in. I was the one who taught her how to take and ride dick. I know all about them sexy ass faces she makes when she's about to nut, the way she shakes uncontrollably when you hit that spot, and them beautiful ass moans. It was me who put that baby in her ass four years ago. It's me who can get the pussy whenever—"

The last of my little spiel never got to come out as it felt like my fucking jaw was being dislocated. I stumbled and tried to catch my fall, but I couldn't do that and block blows from Boss at the same time. Them punches just wouldn't stop coming. Then, when I fell to the ground, I saw another pair of fists and a shoe coming at me. Shit was happening so fast that all I could do was curl up in the fetal position as somebody yelled for Han and Boss to stop.

That was the last thing I heard before I got stomped in the head, and everything went black.

Choyce

*F*or the sixth time today, my call went unanswered. I didn't know if I should've been worried or what. I hadn't talked to Boss since he'd asked me to come to this little cookout he was having a few days ago. Of course, I didn't go, because that wasn't my type of crowd, and I didn't feel safe taking Zamani over that way. I was trying to keep my baby sheltered from some things for as long as I could.

I knew that couldn't have been the reason for Boss not answering my calls for days. I knew he said he was going to be mad if I didn't come, but I ain't think he was literally going to get mad and act like this.

"I know you is not calling that man again," Jamaica snapped at me.

"Maica, I just wanna make sure he's okay," I told her.

"Choyce, you're talking about Boss, the most known, hated, and loved nigga around the city and surrounding areas. If something was wrong with that man, you would've known about it by now. Boss isn't answering, because he doesn't want to, for some reason or another. I know you haven't had a damn boyfriend since the dark ages, but damn, Choyce."

"But what could he be that mad about?" I asked myself more than

Jamaica.

"I don't know, boo, but I do know you're not going to figure it out by sitting here, calling this man nonstop. If you want him to talk to you and get answers, you're going to have to get up and get them," she said.

I had to roll my eyes in annoyance for the simple fact that this was stupid. Boss was a grown ass man, yet he couldn't simply answer the phone and let me know what the hell was up with him.

"Can you keep an eye on Mani for me while I'm gone. I won't be gone long," I asked Jamaica as she lay across my bed, taking pictures on Snapchat.

"Get yo' ass outta here," she said as she literally kicked me out of the bed. "I told you about that shit."

"I'm just asking," I laughed.

"Bye, Choyce. Go get your man, girl," she cheered.

Waving her off with an eye roll, I threw on my shoes so I could get to the bottom of what the hell was going on with Boss. It took me about thirty minutes to get to his house from mine. When I got there, I put the code that he gave me in his gate and was granted access. I didn't see his car in the driveway, but there was a car parked in it, so I proceeded to park and get out.

Taking a deep breath, I rang his doorbell and waited for him an answer. Moments later, somebody opened the door, and I came face to face with some chick I had never seen before. I had to step back and look at the address to make sure I was at the right house.

Who is this bitch?

"Can I help you?" she asked.

She didn't have an attitude or come off rude, but she did look at me with skepticism.

"Uhh, is Boss here?" I asked.

"You're not here to drop off a baby, are you?" she asked through squinted eyes.

"Huh? No, I was—"

"Miss Choyce!" Giselle yelled as she ran down the stairs and straight to me.

"Hi, baby!" I gushed as she hugged me tightly.

"You came to see me? Where's Mani?" Giselle asked as she looked behind me, wondering where her partner in crime was.

"She's at home, sweetie. I'm sorry."

"Aww, that's okay. Maybe next time," she said sweetly.

"Gi-Gi, don't be rude. Let her come in. It's nice to finally put a face to the name. I'm Freedom, Boss's sister."

"Nice to meet you. I've heard a lot about you." I smiled as she stepped to the side so I could me in.

"All good things, I hope. My brother can be a bit of an exaggerator at times," she laughed.

"Definitely. Boss always has nothing but good things to say about you. He's very proud of you," I let her know exactly what her brother told me.

"Awww, look at my big brother. He really does love me," she said as we shared a laugh. "Well, Choyce, his big head self ain't even here. He and Han went to take care of some business. They've been gone for a while, so they should be back soon if you wanna stay here and wait for him," Freedom told me.

"Umm, that's fine. I'll just try to catch up with him another time. I don't wanna—"

"Miss Choyce, pleaseee! Don't leave!" Giselle begged as she grabbed a hold of my hand in her small hands.

"Yes, please, don't leave. I've been trying to meet you for the longest, but I feel like my brother has been hiding you from me. This was nothing but fate," Freedom said.

I silently and quickly weighed out my options as Freedom and Giselle both watched me with hopeful eyes. I did drive all the way out here to talk to Boss, and it would've been defeating the purpose if I'd left.

"Okay, okay."

"Yes!" they both said simultaneously.

"Come on, girl, let's do some girl talk," Freedom said as she grabbed my hand.

She led me up the stairs to her room where she sent Giselle off to her room and shut the door behind us.

"So, did you really meet my brother in the strip club?" she asked as she plopped down on the bed.

Letting out a laugh, I nodded my head. "I sure did. I didn't even know who he was then. I mean, I had heard of him but never really seen him. Imagine my surprise when I found out the nigga I was bumping and grinding on was the infamous Boss of the streets."

"So how long have you been stripping? I tried it a few times back in Louisiana, but I was scared as hell to fully get into it," she said.

"Since I was sixteen, when I had my daughter," I told her. "But that lifestyle is not something you want to get caught up in. It's easy to get into but hard as hell to get out of; the shit will swallow you whole if you let it," I informed her.

"I understand, but my brother loves your daughter. He might not tell you, but I know him, and I also know for a fact that he loves you too," she said.

"I don't know about love. He barely likes my ass," I said through a small laugh.

"No, trust me on this one; he does. I've known my brother all my life, and I've been there through all his drama with women. His last relationship really hurt him. I'm not sure if he told you about Gianna," Freedom said.

"That's Giselle's mom, right?" I asked. "He told me about her little situation, but that's about it," I shrugged.

"Yeah, that's her. Boss really loved her trifling ass, but she turned around and did my brother so dirty. She was fucking our older brother behind his back and ended up getting pregnant. The bitch didn't want Boss to find out, so she went and got a fucking abortion, thinking he would never know. To this day, I don't know if Gianna knows that he knows about the pregnancy," Freedom explained.

"Damn." I whistled. "That's crazy. See, he never told me about that or the fact that you two have an older brother," I said.

Boss always spoke so highly about Freedom, so I thought she was his only sibling. I never knew he had an older brother; never did he speak on him.

"I'm not surprised. Hendrix and Boss have been beefing since the beginning of time. This whole situation with Gianna just kind of brought the shit to a head."

Suddenly, the bedroom door came swinging open, causing both Freedom and me to damn near jump out of our skin.

"Boy, don't be fucking busting in here like that. The hell wrong with you? I swore I locked that door," Freedom fussed.

"This my damn house. I do whatever the hell I wanna do," Boss spoke to her but kept his eyes on me.

I noticed he wasn't giving me the usual look he did when he saw me. This time, his eyes were cold, and his face was hard. I didn't know what to say or how to come at him, so I didn't say anything.

"Boy, say something. Don't just be standing there, staring at her pretty ass," Freedom huffed.

"Fuck you doing here?" he spat.

"I-I. ..." All of a sudden, I was stammering and didn't know what to say.

Boss's whole demeanor was off, and for the life of me, I couldn't figure out why. Just a few days ago, everything between us was good; now, he was acting like somebody I didn't know.

"Umm, I'm going to excuse myself because, obviously, you two need to talk," Freedom said as she got off the bed and walked out of the room.

She doubled back and whispered something in her brother's ear before kissing him on his cheek. She glanced back at me, giving me a small smile before closing the door behind her.

"What did I do?" I questioned, finally finding my voice.

"Why the fuck you ain't tell me that Turk was Zamani's dad?" Boss asked as he stuffed his hands in his pocket.

"Who the hell is Turk?"

I was truly confused. I had heard that name spoken between Boss and Han before, but I didn't know who it was. Now, all of a sudden, Boss was saying that this man was my baby daddy.

"Stop fucking playing with me, Choyce. This man told me to my face, out his own mouth, about how he's been with you—described shit only a nigga who has ever fucked you would know. Then, he proceeded to tell me that he's Zamani's dad, and he can get the pussy whenever he wants to. What type of hoe shit—"

Whap!

Before I knew what the fuck I was doing, I ended up on the other side of the room, slapping the shit out of Boss. After I realized what I had done, I jumped back a little.

"I didn't mean to do that, but don't ever disrespect me, Boston. I haven't been with Turelle, Turk, or whoever the hell he wants to be since before my daughter was born. Me and that man don't even speak to each other. You saw how shit was between us when I first met you.

Think about the shit. Why would I want to be fucking somebody who has never done anything for his child? Turelle is a bitch in every sense of the word. The fact that he even stepped to you with that bullshit proves that," I explained.

I knew, sooner or later, Boss was going to find out, but never would I have thought that Turelle would've been the one to tell him. That nigga had been absent from my daughter's life since before she was even born and denied her to the fullest, but now, all of a sudden, he wanted to tell people she was his daughter. That nigga was ass backwards.

With the speed of lightning, Boss grabbed me by my throat and applied pressure. Not too much to where he was cutting my circulation off but enough to get his point across.

"Don't put yo' muthafuckin hands on me, Choyce. I ain't the type to put my hands on women, but if you wanna get fucked up, I'll be happy to oblige yo' black ass. I don't give a fuck if you ain't talked to Turk in fifteen years. Do you really think I believed for a second you still fucking this nigga? It's the fact that you know this nigga in my camp but never once mentioned that he was Mani's dad. You let that nigga feel like he was doing something when he stepped to me crazy and said some shit you should've told me from the jump!" he said aggressively before letting my throat go.

"How the hell was I supposed to know that we was ... you know? That's not fair, Boss," I sighed.

Okay, maybe just *maybe*, I should've told Boss, but what difference would it have made? What would it have changed? Turelle still wasn't gon' be a part of my daughter's life, and I was going to continue living my life as if he doesn't exist.

"No, what's not fair is you being deceitful and keeping shit from me. You know how I am about that shit."

"So I should've told you; I'm sorry, but I honestly didn't think it would be that big of a deal. Like I said, Turelle and I don't even talk. He—"

"Do you think I give a fuck about any of that shit, Choyce? I know what type of nigga that man is, so I know he ain't shit. Fuck him! This is about you and the fact that you like keeping shit from me, and I don't know if I can trust you! I have a daughter to protect and—"

"And I don't?" I screeched as I cut him off. "Do you really think it was easy for me to welcome you into my daughter's life and let her get used to and attached to you when I didn't even know what the hell was going on between us? Hell, I still don't know what's going on between us!" I exclaimed.

Stuffing both his hands in his pockets, Boss gave me that same cold but blank expression as before. "I think I'm just going to fall back. I got too much shit going on right now, and I don't need any distractions."

I jerked my head back and looked at him to see if he were serious. I was offended as hell to be called a distraction. With a little laugh, I shook my head and walked right past his ass with my head held high. Chasing a nigga was something I had never been good at. If this were what Boss wanted, then fuck it; there was nothing I could really do about it.

Johann

*A*fter dipping out on this little bitch that I had taken to the hotel for a little fuck session, I was thirsty as hell, so I pulled into this gas station to get myself something to drink. I hit the lock on my Range Rover as I made my way into the damn near empty store. I headed straight to the refrigerator section, opening the door to get myself a Sprite out, immediately opening it, and began guzzling it down.

I walked past the cashier and tossed a five-dollar bill on the counter while steadily in motion.

"Keep the change," I told him before walking right out the door.

Before I could hit the lock on my truck, a face in one of the cars at the pump caught my eye. Some lil' ugly nigga was pumping the gas, but it wasn't him that I was worried about. Twisting the cap on my pop bottle, I went straight for the car. As if she could sense me, Freedom looked up at me looking like she had just been caught with her hand in the cookie jar.

I reached for the car door handle, but she quickly hit the locks before I could answer it.

Here we go.

Sighing in annoyance, I prepared myself for the scene that I knew was about to take place.

141

"Get out the damn car," I said as calmly as I could.

"Gon', Han, I'm not in the mood for your shit tonight," Freedom called herself warning me.

"Aye, what is you doing!" The little nigga she was with tried to puff out his chest.

Ignoring him, I just reached for the gun I always kept on me and busted the window out. Freedom's crazy ass didn't even look fazed. I didn't know whether I was tripping or not, but I could've sworn I seen a little smirk on her face.

"Allow me to assist you," I said as I reached in, unlocked the door, and snatched it open.

"Stop it, Johann! You always gotta take shit to the next extreme!" she yelled at me as I yanked her dumb ass out the car.

"Freedom, you—"

"Little nigga, if you wanna keep that breath in yo' body and yo' heart pumping, I advise you to back the fuck up," I let him know with nothing but venom dripping from each word I spoke.

"I'm so sorry, Trey. I'll pay for it to get fixed; just, please, get back in the car," Freedom warned him.

I looked at her like she was stupid when she told this nigga she would pay for his window. They both had me fucked up on this beautiful night. She was never going to see this nigga again, and I was going to make sure of it.

"Get yo' dumb ass in the car." I shoved her towards my car.

"Stop talking to me like I'm your child, Johann. I'm grown as hell," she said as she snatched away from me.

"Oh yeah? Thanks to you, I don't have any of my fucking kids," I spat at her before I knew it.

Freedom stopped dead in her tracks and looked at me with nothing but hurt and pain in her eyes before she took off in the opposite direction. I was silently kicking myself for saying that shit.

"Dom. ..."

I tried to stop her, but she took off running like somebody was chasing her. I was just going to have to tell Boss what the fuck was going on between his sister and me because she was a half second away from me beating her ass. She really had my ass out here in the middle of the night, chasing her ass, literally.

"Stop, man! Fuck wrong with you?" I yelled as I caught her ass.

"Get the fuck off me, Johann! Let me go! I'm sick of you blaming me for that shit. It wasn't my fault," Freedom cried as she tried to get away from me.

I had no choice but to pick her up and throw her over my shoulder, because she wasn't going without a fight. I walked her over to my truck and put her bratty ass in the back seat where I had the child lock on since she wanted to act like a damn kid.

Had me coming all out of body.

When I got in the car, she was back there pouting with her lip poked out as the tears fell down her face. I quickly turned around to back out of my parking spot. She knew I hated when she did that crying shit.

"Take me home," she said softly.

"Okay," I responded.

"Take me to my brother's house, Johann," she said. "I'm not playing with you."

I just turned the music up on her ass as I headed for my destination. Suddenly, a thought hit my mind.

"Fuck was you doing with that nigga?" I questioned as I turned the music down. "Yo' brother know you out here with these random ass niggas? You gave that nigga my pussy?" I asked all in one breath.

Freedom just sucked her teeth as she adjusted herself in her seat with her arms still folded. She rolled her eyes and looked out my tinted windows as if I weren't talking to her.

"What I do, and who I do it with, is not your concern. You don't want me, remember? Besides, you can't question me about shit when you smell like you just crawled from between a bitch's legs," Freedom said as she gave me a look that was icy enough to freeze hell over.

"Guess what? I did," I told her.

I glanced in the mirror just as the look of hurt appeared on her face before it turned to anger.

"Let me out this truck! You so damn disrespectful!" she yelled as she tried to yank open the door, but it wouldn't budge.

"You wanna know what else?" I egged on. "The shit was so damn mediocre that I couldn't even bust a damn nut. For some reason, the whole time she was riding my dick, another chick was on my mind," I told her honestly.

That was the God-honest truth. The whole time I was trying to get my rocks off with another bitch, thoughts of Freedom kept invading my mind. Ever since she reappeared on the scene, all I could think about was her. Even though I hadn't been inside her walls in years, Freedom was like a drug to me. I knew that she was no good for me, but I just couldn't leave her alone. I was addicted to her. Literally, after one taste of her, my body started craving her.

Not just her sweet pussy, but everything about Freedom was so addictive. Her smile, her touch, her warmth, but even more importantly, her love. She had this aura about her that I hadn't found in anybody else.

Of course, our shit wasn't perfect; we fought like cats and dogs, and the way we went about things in the past was fucked up, but the love I had for Freedom was something that came around only once in a lifetime. Even still, I knew that we could never be together. Our past was too fucked up, and I would never be beefed out with my best friend over the issue. So, the only thing I could do was love her from a distance. Was the shit ideal? Hell no, but sometimes, you had to do what you had to do.

"I said take me home, Johann. You don't listen," Freedom huffed as we pulled up to my house.

I just ignored her and kept pulling into the driveway. I got out opened her door for her, but I stopped her from getting out.

"Move—"

"Aye, just hear me out real quick," I told her as I stood between her legs. Of course, her stubborn ass refused to look at me, but I ain't care. "Dom. ... Freedom, I'm sorry. For everything. I ain't mean that shit I said back at the gas station. I was just saying shit to make you feel the way I felt when I saw you with another nigga. It's not your fault I don't have either of my kids; it's my fault. My bullshit, lies, and games were what caused me to not only lose both of my children or my daughter's mother, but you as well. If I would've just kept shit one hunnit from the beginning, none of this shit would've went down the way it did."

I finally had her full attention, and she was looking at me very attentively.

"I love you; don't ever doubt that shit. A nigga really crazy over you if you ain't know. It's just we can't be together. Not only am I no good for you. but we're no good for each other. You make me crazy and be having me out here on some other shit, and I don't like that. You gon' always be my lil' baby, and I'm still putting bullets in *any* nigga that you *think* you gon' fuck with," I told her honestly.

"Whatever, Johann," she said lowly as she pushed me away from her. "I don't care about none of that. I'm just ready to go to bed," she said in the same low tone as she walked up to the door, never turning around.

I just ran my hands down my face as I shook my head. This dealing with females shit was stressful as hell. This was exactly why I just fucked broads then went on to the next one. This was exactly why.

Choyce

$\mathcal{I}$ sat with both of my legs on either side of the bench as I counted how much money I had made so far. Ever since I had stopped fucking with Boss, I had thrown myself back into stripping. I couldn't lie, his slick ass had thrown me off my game and kept me away from the club, but now, I was back, and I was better.

"So you haven't heard from him at all? Like, he hasn't tried to reach out to you?" Buffy asked as she touched up her lipstick.

I didn't have any real friends outside of Jamaica and Buffy. Those two were the only ones that I let get close to me because I knew just how fake bitches were. The moment I walked through the doors of this club after being off the scene for a few weeks due to Boss keeping me away, Buffy immediately knew something was wrong and wanted all the tea.

"Nope," I said, without losing count. "Fuck him. I'm one step closer to reaching my goal, and I don't need any distractions as he puts it."

When Boss stood there and called me a distraction, I didn't know how to feel. I still didn't know how to feel, honestly. He was the one who'd stepped to me, he pursued me, and he wasted my time—not the other way around. So, for him to call me a distraction was a definite slap in the face.

To make matters even worse, he allowed my daughter to get attached to him, and I'd gotten attached to Giselle as well. I was missing her something terrible, but because her Daddy was a dumb ass, I was forced to be missing out on her beautiful self.

"Babe," Buffy sighed as she turned to look at me. "You know I'm not one to spread shit around when I hear it, but you my boo, so I'm going to put you on to some shit," she said.

"What?"

"I heard that trifling ass baby mama of his is back around. Now, I had to check my sources and info before I stepped to you with this shit, but the two of them have definitely been seen out together. Apparently, she's off the drugs and all of a sudden remembered she had a daughter or whatever. I thought it was a bunch of nothing until you told me that y'all wasn't fucking with each other no more. Now, I'm starting to put two and two together," she informed me.

Now, I could've sat up here and acted like I wasn't fazed about what I just heard, but that wasn't me. I was human, and I had emotions no matter how hard I fought to not let them show. That was some pretty interesting information Buffy just put me on to. That nigga was acting as if he was so over and done with his baby mama, but now, they were a happy family.

"What can I say, Buff? He obviously didn't want me, and now, we know why. I wish he would've just kept it real with me and not wasted my time, acting like he was really feeling me when he wasn't. I wish them nothing but the best, though," I shrugged.

Just as Buffy was about to say something, two dancers that neither of us cared for walked in. Buffy eyed them down, and I just rolled my eyes in annoyance as they came in, being loud as hell, just doing anything to get some attention.

"Girl, did you see that fine ass nigga Han out there? I'm about to take his ass to one of them private rooms and straight snatch his soul," the one we called Kitty said.

"You do that, boo, but I want that fine ass friend of his. That nigga Boss is something out of this world," the other one known as Seduction said.

I looked over in Buffy's direction, and she shook her head at me as if to tell me not to react.

"I heard he got a big dick," Kitty said.

Very big, bitch.

"I'll let you know for sure when I finish riding the fuck out of it." Seduction popped her big ass lips as they shared a high five.

Bitch, you could never.

"Both of y'all hoes 'bout dumb as fuck. Especially yo' plastic ass," Buffy said to Seduction. "All that silicone you got in yo' ass and titties must've traveled up to ya brain. Boss would never fuck a raggedy ass bitch like you. Hoe, you pushing thirty and still showing off yo' fake ass and botched titties in the club. It's been time for you to give up the gig, hoe," Buffy went in on her, and I couldn't help but let out a little laugh.

"The fuck you laughing for, Choyce? You got beef or something? You had your chance with the nigga, but you flopped. Clearly, you wasn't shit but a easy fuck for the nigga. He got what he wanted out of you and dropped you like a bad habit. You had to be smoking dope if you thought he was going to take you out the club and wife you up. Boss don't love bitches; even I know that," Seduction said.

"Hold up, bitch. The fuck you coming at her for when I'm the one who sent for you. You talking about somebody got beef, but you clearly feeling some type of way about my girl right now. Yo' washed up ass better watch who you coming at," Buffy spoke up in my defense.

"What are you? Her bodyguard or something?" Kitty asked.

"Her friend. What the fuck are you? Her flunky or something, ... bitch?" Buffy said.

"Buff, come on. These bitches not even worth you getting all bent out of shape over. Let's just go out here and make some money. You know we the top money makers in this bitch; we make more in one night than they do in a week; that's why they really mad," I said to Buffy.

"Well, would you look at that? Who knew her stuck up ass had it in her to talk shit. The whole time, I thought this bitch was fucking retarded," Seduction laughed.

"I heard her daughter was too. This hoe act all high and mighty, but she don't even know who her dumb ass daughter's daddy is," Kitty laughed.

"Fuck you just say?" I stopped dead in my tracks.

"And I'm not going to try to stop her from beating yo' ass. You deserve this beat down, hoe," Buffy said she stepped to the side.

"You heard me," Kitty said.

"Kit, chill out. You went too far, talking about her daughter," Seduction cowered down.

"I was just saying what everybody else around here been—"

Kitty's bullshit was cut off by my fist connecting with her mouth. I wasn't the type to fight unless I had to, but this bitch crossed the line when she brought my child into some grown-up shit. I would never talk about somebody's child just because I had a beef with them.

"Beat her ass, Choyce! Beat that bitch's ass!" Buffy coached in the background.

"Ahh!" I screamed out when I felt Kitty's stiletto nails digging in my face.

Instead of stopping, that just made me want to beat her ass more. I had so much anger and frustration built up inside of me that it was just boiling over, all of a sudden. I used my weight to swing Kitty around and get her on the ground. She had a death grip on my hair, so we both ended up falling, but as luck would have it, I got on top and proceeded to beat her ass.

"Okay, Choyce. That's enough; she's bleeding. Choyce! Choyce! Calm down, babe, it's okay!" Buffy yelled as she tried to help one of the guards break it up.

When I snapped out of it, I realized that I now had an audience. Almost all the dancers, even the owner of the club, were in the room with wide eyes. Nobody had ever seen this side of me before. This was one of the main reasons I didn't like to get angry; I turned into a completely different person.

Everybody thought that because I let a lot of shit go and didn't get worked up or aggressive that I was soft or scary. That couldn't have been further from the truth. I grew up in a home where I literally had to fight every day of my life. My anger used to be crazy until I had my daughter and calmed my ass down.

Snatching away from the guard, I went over to the locker and took out all my belongings. I threw my yoga pants on over my thong and threw my jacket on before picking up my gym bag. I rushed out the door, not saying anything to anyone.

"Choyce!" the owner called after me.

I just ignored his ass and kept it pushing. I really ain't have shit to say to anyone at this point. I was embarrassed for showing my ass like that when I should've just taken my own advice and walked away from the bullshit.

My head was so fucked up that I did about sixty home, the whole way. All I wanted to do was soak in the tub so I wouldn't be sore in the morning and cuddle up with my baby, but she was spending the weekend with her god-mom so that plan was a dub. I had a mind to stop by Jamaica's house and pick Zamani up, but I knew Jamaica wouldn't have that.

I sluggishly got out of my car and walked up to my front door while trying to get my house key together. I heard something behind me, so I turned around to see what it was, which was a mistake on my part. Before I could even let out a scream, my attacker grabbed me by the throat and started squeezing. I tried to fight for my life, but the more I fought, the harder he squeezed. Just when I thought I was going to die, I was hit over the head, being knocked unconscious.

Boss

$\mathcal{I}$t was only one dimly lit light throughout the whole empty warehouse. I stood back in the shadows of the darkness and watched as a bloody nigga hung from the ceiling by the chains wrapped around his wrist. Slowly emerging from the dark, I walked up to him, making myself noticed in the light. His eyes got wide as best as they could even though they were bloody and swollen.

"Bo-Boss. Please," he said weakly.

Taking my jacket off, I threw it on the ground before removing my hunting knife. I slowly walked around him, shaking my head in pity.

"Honesty, … loyalty, … respect, … common sense. That's just a few of the things yo' bitch ass lacks," I told him as I made my way back in front of him.

This was clearly one of the moments that my pops had been telling me about. He always said niggas will love you to your face but hate you behind your back. He always told me that the power I was going to possess was going to be a blessing but a curse at the same time.

He wasn't lying.

"Come on, B. I-I ain't mean to. You-you know my loyalty is to you, but-but—"

"But what, muthafucka?" I yelled. "Ain't no buts in this shit! You think it's okay to bite the muthafucking hand that feeds you? I put a lot of bread in yo' pockets, fed yo' fam, helped yo' brother out when he got in that little situation, and even paid for yo' sister's funeral. This how the fuck you pay me back? By stealing from me?" I was trying to contain the beast I had living inside of me, but he was fighting hard to set himself free.

I had gotten to the bottom of the situation with Juarez and his shit being short. I thought that nigga was just pulling my leg and trying to one up me until I checked into the situation like I said I would. Come to find out, a nigga in my own camp was stealing my shit. Kimbae was in charge of drop-offs and pick-ups. In order for a nigga to have that job, I had to have a lot of trust for him. Obviously, that shit came back to bite me in the ass.

This nigga was taking shit out of the stash when he was supposed to be transporting the shit. What these niggas I had around me didn't know was I had eyes and ears everywhere. I didn't care how much I claimed I trusted a muthafucka, I ain't put shit past anybody. If I didn't trust the nigga I came from the same nut sack as, then I couldn't trust nobody.

"He had me by the balls, B. That dirty muthafucka had my freedom in his hand. He said he would lock me up if I ain't do it," Kimbae cried.

"Who the fuck is he?" I spat.

"Some cop nigga; he's a dirty ass cop. He always come around fucking with us and asking questions. He busted me one night and asked me if I worked for you. I thought the shit was weird, so I ain't say shit. He laughed and said he already knew the answer. He said, in exchange for my freedom, I had to basically become an informant. I wasn't fucking with that shit, so I tried to avoid his ass, but he came around and fucked me up with these big goon looking niggas. He told me if I ain't steal the shit, he was going to lock my black ass up for the rest of my life. You know I can't let my mama lose another child, especially with her taking my sister dying real bad," he explained.

Hendrix.

"So, what you're telling me is you folded under pressure? It's crazy that this nigga been fucking with y'all, but nobody thought to tell me the shit so I could get it handled. That's where you fucked up, Kimbae," I told him as I examined the knife.

The whole time I was interrogating his ass, my phone was vibrating in my pants pocket. I was already in the middle of something, so I had no choice but to ignore it. I was sure the shit wasn't that important anyway. Nobody that ever called me wanted shit.

"I tried, man. B-Boss. You—ahh!"

I was tired of listening to the bullshit, so I shut his ass up—for good. I took my knife and stabbed his bitch ass right in his stomach before gutting him like he was some damn catfish. Stepping back, I looked at my handiwork. I hadn't done shit like this in years.

Maybe Han was right; I had gotten too comfortable, and these niggas forgot just how looney I was. Niggas out here were thinking that I had gotten soft or something, so I was going to have to show them that old nigga inside of me never died. I just kept his ass locked up because they wouldn't know what to do with that side of me.

That shit was a wrap, though. I was back on my bullshit and planned to get these niggas back in order, one by one. Starting with Hendrix. Brother or not, that nigga had to go. It was going to break my mama's heart, but she would be alright. She had two other kids out here, so what was losing one going to hurt?

Walking over to the sink, I washed Kimbae's blood from my hands. Once again, my phone started vibrating in my pocket. Drying my hands, I pulled it out but not in time to answer the call. I checked it to see I had a few text messages from an unknown number, as well as from Han, along with a missed call from my right-hand man. Clicking on Han's message, I opened it.

Han: *Aye, I need to talk to you about some shit.*

Checking the rest of my messages, I clicked on the texts from the unknown number.

"What the fuck!"

It was some pictures of Gianna with a battered and bloody face with a gun to her head. There was a look of horror on her face, and I felt my heart drop to my stomach. Suddenly, somebody called me from a private number.

"Yeah?" I answered skeptically.

"If you wanna see Choyce again, you better listen the fuck up and follow my directions. Try any slick shit, and this bitch is done for," the unknown person said as they disguised their voice.

Choyce?

I surely thought they were calling about Gianna. This nigga had to be a dumb ass because he ain't even know who the fuck he had taken while trying to fuck with me. All of a sudden, I heard some commotion in the background on the other end of the phone. It was followed by a loud scream that caused me to pull my phone away from my ear.

"Boss! Please, help!"

That was definitely Choyce crying out for me. Now, a nigga was stuck and confused. A muthafucka was really trying me, and that wasn't the safest thing to do. Now, I had a big ass dilemma on my hands. I could try to run and save my past or save the person I saw a future with. Both Gianna and Choyce's lives were in my hands, and I wasn't sure if I could save them both.

What the fuck am I going to do?

TO BE CONTINUED

CONTACT CHARMANIE SAQUEA

Facebook: Charmanie Saquea

Twitter: __saqueaaa

Instagram: iam.saquea

Readers Group: Charmanie's Queendom

Text CHARM to 42828 to stay up to date on future releases

Looking for a publishing home?

Royalty Publishing House, Where the Royals reside, is accepting submissions for writers in the urban fiction genre. If you're interested, submit the first 3-4 chapters with your synopsis to submissions@royaltypublishinghouse.com.

Check out our website for more information: www.royaltypublishinghouse.com.

Text ROYALTY to 42828 to join our mailing list!

To submit a manuscript for our review, email us at submissions@royaltypublishinghouse.com

Text RPHCHRISTIAN to 22828 for our CHRISTIAN ROMANCE novels!

Text RPHROMANCE to 22828 for our INTERRACIAL ROMANCE novels!

Do You Like CELEBRITY GOSSIP?

Check Out QUEEN DYNASTY!
Visit Our Site: www.thequeendynasty.com

Get LiT!

Download the LiT eReader app today and enjoy exclusive content, free books, and more

CPSIA information can be obtained
at www.ICGtesting.com
Printed in the USA
LVOW10s1721020518
575706LV00016B/1248/P